Lessons in Love

A Romantic Comedy

S.L. Scott

Cover Design: RBA Designs - New Cover 2025
Editing & Proofreading: Marla Esposito - Proofing with Style
Editing: Virginia Tesi Carey

FOLLOW ME

To keep up to date with her writing and more, visit S.L. Scott's website: **www.slscottauthor.com**

To receive the newsletter about all of her publishing adventures, free books, giveaways, steals and more:

https://geni.us/SLScottNL

Follow on IG: https://geni.us/IGSLS
Follow me on TikTok: https://geni.us/SLTikTok
Follow on Bookbub: https://geni.us/SLScottBB

Also by S.L. Scott

Called **"The Most Romantic Book Ever,"** We Were Once, is available and FREE in Kindle Unlimited.

We Were Once

The international sensation, **Best I Ever Had**, has won readers over and is available in ebook, audio, and paperback, and Free in Kindle Unlimited.

Best I Ever Had

Audiobooks on Audible - CLICK HERE

Peachtree Pass Series (Stand-alones)

Long Time Coming /Lead Me Knot /Small Town Frenzy

The Westcott Series (Stand-alones)

Swear on My Life / Never Saw You Coming

Forgot to Say Goodbye / When I Had You

Never Have I Ever / Speak of the Devil - Faris Family

Hard to Resist Series (Stand-Alones)

The Resistance / The Reckoning

The Redemption / The Revolution / The Rebellion

The Crow Brothers (Stand-Alones)

Spark / Tulsa / Rivers / Ridge

The Crow Brothers Box Set

DARE - A Rock Star Hero (Stand-Alone)

New York Love Stories (Stand-Alones)

Never Got Over You / The One I Want / Crazy in Love

Head Over Feels / It Started with a Kiss

The Everest Brothers (Stand-Alones)

Everest / Bad Reputation / Force of Nature

The Everest Brothers Box Set

The Kingwood Series

SAVAGE / SAVIOR / SACRED / FINDING SOLACE

The Kingwood Series Box Set

Playboy in Paradise Series

Falling for the Playboy / Redeeming the Playboy

Loving the Playboy

Playboy in Paradise Box Set

Stand-Alone Books

Best I Ever Had

We Were Once

Along Came Charlie

Missing Grace

Finding Solace

Until I Met You

Drunk on Love

Lost in Translation

Sleeping with Mr. Sexy

Morning Glory

For the lovers and dreamers, the peppermint mochas, and the coffee creamers: I hope you enjoy this romantic comedy as much as I enjoyed writing it.

Prologue

Blondes
Vodka soda.

Brunettes.
Rum and Coke.

Redheads.
Amaretto Sour.

Highlights.
Mojito.

Lowlights.
Beer.

Knotted on Top.
Margaritas.

Pulled Back.
Gin and tonic.

Bobs.
Moscow Mules.

Long.
Champagne.

Short.
Tequila shots.

Shoulder-length.
Sex on the Beach.

Chapter One

This story is told from the Hero's POV.

As a dude, I know too much about women's hair. But in my line of work, it's a bonus. I can call it the second I see them. One quick glance and I know a woman sporting bangs and long layers is going to want something strong like they are, but independent and free-spirited like they wish they were. I'd wager on a Whiskey Sour.

No matter what their hairstyle, the one thing all women have in common is sex. Yup, sex. You might say that sounds trite, even obvious, but it's true. There's a basic need, a desire that the right cocktail with the right opportunity at the right time can release, making the most put together woman come undone.

Back to me, which is how I like it, that and a good bob on my knob. I'm the owner, Hardy Richard. Hence the name above the door—Hardy's Hideaway, where cocktails are served alongside a good helping of cock tales. Sure I could have gone for the obvious, but Dick's was already taken. The owner of that bar a few blocks from here doesn't even see the irony in his name. I do, and I own every inch of my iron.

Tucked down a street near the Brooklyn Bridge, the Hideaway attracts not just Manhattanites but locals too. The clientele changes often, each night bringing a parade of the lonely, the content, the happy, the sad, the partiers, and the overt. Women in every shape and size frequent my bar looking for a good time with their boyfriends, girlfriends, husbands, wives, partners, significant others, regular hook ups, and strangers.

They're all here for the same reasons—a good time and a great fuck. The Hideaway is happy to provide both. Our customers are left satisfied because we're more than just bartenders. We're therapists. We're life coaches. We're teachers. We're lovers. We're sexual healers. Here, under the dim lights, we're gods. My team is gifted, leaving our patrons smiling and wanting more. Word of mouth has worked its way around the five boroughs and business is booming. Our motto is threefold. The customer is always right, they always come, and they always come back. Goals we strive for night after night.

We're not particularly hidden being a corner bar, but once you cross that threshold, this is a place where you get to be who you are when you're alone, the person you want to be, a better version of yourself. No one here judges. I love watching the transformation throughout the evening. They come in here after work or a long day running around doing what unsupervised women do, whether that be—playing mommy to the brood at home or to the man paying them big bucks—this is their escape, where they congregate to wind down.

I wipe down the bar top and throw new coasters down for the after happy hour crowd. We call it the second wave. I look up just as a dark brunette stands a foot back analyzing the liquor bottles lined up against the mirror behind me. Every strand is perfectly in place and pulled back so taut it looks professionally styled. *Gimlet.* She's holding onto her designer purse like we're in a house of thieves. She doesn't realize it yet, but the only thing we're looking to steal is that tightly wound good girl image she's projecting. I'd love to see her lipstick smeared outside her lined lips. I bet she has a solid handful of hair to pull too. Afterwards, I wouldn't let her put it back up. I'd make her walk out of here freshly fucked with her hair down, loose around her shoulders. She'd feel too good to care how she looked. *Too crude?* I should start with her first drink. "What can I get you?"

"Gimlet."

It's almost too easy. Wonder if she is.

"Coming right up." And boy am I. I grab a glass from the cooler and go for the chilled gin—top shelf, like her. My gaze relishes her curves she's trying to hide behind that expensive, but unflattering suit. Charcoal gray. She should never try to look like a man when she's one of the most beautiful women I've ever seen. I won't make her compete in a man's world. I'll show her she can be in charge while I have her submitting to me. Sounds like an oxymoron, but trust me, I know what she really needs. At least when it comes to the bar or the bedroom.

Or the office.

Or the backroom.

Or the bathroom.

Hell, I'll fuck her on top of this bar if that's what gets her off.

I pour Rose's Lime Juice, squeeze fresh lime, and gin into a shaker. With my arms above my right shoulder, I shake. Keeping my eyes on her, she looks up, watching the shaker held in my hands. "I'm Hardy," I introduce myself.

"As in Hardy's Hideaway?"

"The very one." I pour her drink into the martini glass and add a slice of lime to the lip. "What's your name?"

"Constance."

Holding my hand out, she slips hers into mine. She doesn't have to, but I know it's coming. Her grip begins to compete. It's a control issue I'm happy to help with and relinquish to her. "Constance is a pretty name."

Her fingers smooth hair that's already smoothed, her gaze dipping away as embarrassment colors her cheeks. Now this is unexpected. I want more. I want to watch that blush spread across her bare chest when she rides me and then down her spine when I take her from behind. And before you get all riled up over the sex talk, you should know I enjoy sex. I like to make love. I love to fuck. I like the foreplay. I enjoy the after play. A little cuddling is good after a romp in the sack. Kisses are fine as long as emotions are kept at bay. I'm not broken. I'm not recovering from heartbreak, and I'm not pining over a lost love. Nope. I just like the simple act of connecting with another human on a raw and carnal level. I like the euphoria of hitting that peak and then tumbling down into a state of satiation with bones of jelly and a mind free from daily troubles. I like giving that same freedom to women who seem to struggle to find it.

So I don't need a lecture on how I'm heartless. I'm not. I've been in relationships and they're just not for me. But I still enjoy bonding physically with women. Many women.

Sitting down on a barstool, she wraps her fingers around the stem of the glass. I watch as she takes her first sip, her eyes dipping closed. Bliss lingers on her lips, glistening against her pinot noir colored mouth. Her tongue slips out to taste the tart liquid. Long, dark lashes lift and she says, "It's perfect."

"That's what I strive for."

"You should strive for something more tangible."

"Don't underestimate the perfection of a good cocktail."

Holding her drink up, she says, "Touché." After taking a deeper sip this time, she smiles sweetly, but mischievously. "You have customers, Hardy."

I like the way she says my name, an upswing on the ending. I can't wait to hear it two octaves higher rolling off her tongue. "Just whistle if you need me."

Nodding, she tends to the phone that lights up in front of her. I leave her be, tending to the other ladies looking for love, or drinks. "What can I get you?"

Light blond. Fake—pretty much everything, but it's working for her. "Are you available?"

"Are you asking for you, or *for a friend?*"

She bites her lower lip, leaving tracks in her bright pink lipstick. I've had that shade wrapped around my cock before. I'm feeling something moodier tonight—to be specific—pinot noir. I purse my lips, and then smile. "Unfortunately, I have a long shift ahead of me."

"I heard rumors about your long shaft." She covers her mouth with her hand and giggles. "I mean, shift." Her flirting is lacking, but she seems nice enough. "Guess I'm out of luck tonight."

"I'm still serving, if you're thirsty."

Dragging her tongue over her bottom lip, she replies, "So thirsty. I could just guzzle you down."

My cock stirs.

There's a point in the evening, early on, like now, just after seven when I like to fuck. I'm not sure if it's the excitement of what's to come for the night, hopefully me, or the thought of opportunity presenting itself. But almost every shift, my little buddy becomes my hard as a rock friend and is easily tempted the first chance he gets. I've learned to curb the craving. I may like sex, a lot, but I'm not easy. "Something to drink?"

"Sex on the Beach." Pure sugar. No subtlety. Like the woman in front of me.

I've had sex with two women—together and separately—in the same night. I'm not ashamed of my sexual history or my sex drive. I'm happy to please and be pleasured. Like I said, it's part of what makes us human and connects us on a deeper level. But if I was to compare, I'm in the mood for spicier notes with more depth. Tonight I'd rather have one strong drink than a slew of cheap ones. I may have gotten Constance's drink order right but I called it all wrong when it came to her. I must remedy this, and not with candy-coated fruit punch drinks.

I place the drink in front of her, and then slide down to the other end of the bar. I stop in front of Constance, someone I consider a top shelf among call drinks. "Ready for another?"

The glass is emptied and pushed toward me. "I need to close out."

"What?" No. "Leaving so soon?"

"My date cancelled, so I'm going to call it a night and go home."

"Stay. Drinks on me." Literally, if I'm lucky.

She smiles and if I'm not mistaken, she's about to take

me up on my offer. Looking at what I suspect is the time on her phone, she acquiesces. "Okay, maybe one more."

I'm getting a clean glass before the words leave her mouth, and ask, "Boyfriend?"

"Who?"

"The chump who stood you up. Is he your boyfriend?"

"I don't think I've heard the word chump used in person or ever."

"Eh, I was being polite. Asshole is what I was really thinking."

While I shake the fresh cocktail, she laughs a little, then with melancholy tainting our good time, she says, "No, he's not my boyfriend. I wish. This is the second time we've tried to get together and he's cancelled."

"Asshole."

"Lawyer."

"Same thing." She laughs louder this time, and I like the sound of it. Wanting to see her smile more, I say, "Don't wish on falling stars. Wish on rising suns. There's more hope to be found there."

"That's beautiful."

"You're beautiful. He's a fool for standing you up."

I fill the martini glass, then because I find her so damn attractive sitting there with her heart invested in something it shouldn't, I suggest, "I have this premium gin you should try."

Tapping the glass, she eyes it. "If it's not in here, why are you holding back the good stuff?"

I spend more time than I probably should with her when I know there are others waiting on drinks. "Next one. I promise."

"I'm going to hold you to that." She takes the glass and sips. "Mmmm. You are a very talented bartender."

"Bartending's not my only talent."

Resting her chin on her hand, her eyebrows rise. "Oh really?"

Constance is quite the conundrum. A Gimlet Girl never blushes like she just did. Then for her to turn around and speak words in seductive purrs. She's a mystery I want to unravel.

Unfortunately my name is being called back to tend to Sex on the Beach. Since I never told her my name and she's using it like she's got stock in it, I'm guessing my reputation brought her in tonight. I'm not sure what's keeping her here though after making it clear it's a no-go. I tell Constance, "I'll be back." I tap the bar top and walk back down to the other end. "You ready to close your tab?"

She looks offended. "No. I was hoping for another."

"Sure thing."

"Yes, I am."

"I appreciate the offer," I say, pouring the drink straight out of the premixed batch I made earlier. "But I'm gonna have to pass tonight." Firm and clear.

She shrugs. "No problem. Now that I know where this place is, I'll be back."

I set the drink down and busy myself with other customers. I thought this would be a slower Monday, but apparently the whole city decided to stop in tonight.

Chapter Two

The Hideaway is packed. I look out at a sea of pretty people and smile. It will be a good night for business. It will be a great night for hookups. I've got Eddie and Will working behind the bar with me to keep up with orders.

I notice an empty glass a few barstools down and make sure I'm the one that fills it. "How are you doing, Constance?"

"The Gimlets are great." Her mood has improved significantly, and I like the way she's looking at me.

She's funny. "How about you?"

"Feeling . . . crowded in." She glances over her shoulder before returning her eyes to me while a finger runs over the top of the glass. "I've been thinking that I might like a taste of that gin you mentioned earlier."

"I can arrange that," I reply, getting closer and making sure only she hears me. "We have a rule here at The Hideaway though."

Leaning in, she asks, "What's that?"

"We keep the good stuff in the back."

A smile tickles her lips and a giggle slips out. "Am I allowed back there? I'd hate to get you in trouble with the boss."

Fuuuuck. She's playing a game with me. I knew I liked her. "Could be risky." It's good to be the boss right now.

Sliding off the stool, she grabs her purse, and says, "Risks are just dares you were brave enough to take. Are you brave enough to take me, Hardy?"

"I can take you." Over my knee. From behind. Sprawled out across my desk. Against the liquor locker. My cock pings against my jeans, and I shout behind me, "Cover me, Eddie."

"Gotcha covered." He eyes Constance and gives me a look of approval.

I toss my towel in the corner before I walk around and hold out my elbow for her to take. Her slender fingers wrap around my arm and we walk through the crowd toward the hall that leads to the offices. A door is pushed open and the crowds and music fade behind us. I say, "Right down here." I pull my keys out and unlock the door.

Letting her go first, she steps in and looks around the large space. "It's big."

"You haven't seen anything yet."

With a laugh, she leans her fine ass against the desk and I can't say I disapprove of this—her ass on my desk. My dick is starting to ache. "You're very good with the innuendoes."

"I'm good with a lot of things. Want me to show you?"

All the bravado that she carried in here starts to sink. "I don't do this."

That's okay. I'm kind of liking the banter enough to continue, "Do what, Constance? Taste good gin?"

Her smile is back, but it's a weaker version of the one

that lit up the bar earlier. Her hand waves between us. "This. Did you make that last drink stronger?"

"Despite what you might think, I don't get women drunk to get laid. I don't have to."

"I'm sorry. I didn't mean—"

Moving in, I take hold of her flailing hands, and still them, hoping to reassure her. "It's okay. You're nervous. I get it. We don't have to do anything but taste some gin together. Would you like that?"

She blows out a breath, and nods. "I'd like that, but not much. I'm feeling lightheaded."

Our bodies are close, her knees against my legs. "We can do this another time."

When she looks up at me, I can see the trust in her eyes. "I want to be here."

"Okay. Be here with me." Not a question. A request.

Her voice softens, her body following suit. "Did you know I'd end up back here?"

"No. But it doesn't change the fact that I hoped you would."

Her smile grows and she stands. Giving me one easy search of the eyes, she moves and I step back, letting her walk around the office freely. "This place must see a lot of action?"

"It does." Honest. No apologies.

An amused scoff whips through her lips. "You're kind of arrogant."

"You're very pretty."

The shyness from earlier returns, but she pretends to own the compliment. For someone as beautiful as she is, I would think compliments are commonplace, but by her reaction, I get the feeling she doesn't receive many. Tapping the top of the desk, she asks, "How much action has this desk seen?"

"Too much." Honest. No apologies.

She turns, so I give her space and retrieve the gin from the liquor locker. Touching the chair, she asks, "How about this chair?"

"More than the desk." Honest. No apologies. When I have the bottle in hand, I waggle it for her to see. "Got it."

Constance is keeping herself entertained by trying to find a surface that hasn't been fucked on, under, or over. "The loveseat?"

"I can't even talk about the deviant acts that have taken place there." Honest. No apologies.

"Deviant? I'm very intrigued."

I take the shots I just poured and hand her one. "The most baseline sexual acts you can think of and I've done them in this room." Honest. No apologies.

"Will you do me in this room?"

Surprised by her initiative, my attention lands firmly on her. "My pleasure is your pleasure."

She sips the gin shot and sets it on the desk. "That's good. Smoother than I expected. How about you?"

"I'll let you determine that." I shoot the shot and set the glass down. "Take off your jacket, Constance."

With her eyes latched onto mine, she lets the jacket slide down the arms of her hot pink silky shirt. Being careful not to wrinkle it, she hangs it over the back of one of the chairs. "Now what?"

"Why'd you come to The Hideaway tonight?"

The Gimlet speaks for her. "My college roommate has known you since the summer. Katie O'Dowd."

The name brings back memories, memories I'm probably okay not recalling. "Katie O'Dowd. I remember her. I

14

fucked her in the bathroom. She liked the door unlocked so people could walk in and see us."

"That's what she said."

"Is that what you're into? Do you like to be watched?"

"No. I don't know. I don't think so. What about you?"

The stammering is a clear sign I've touched on something that makes her uncomfortable. I attempt to get her back on track. "Not really. What brought you here?"

"A date, like I said earlier."

"No," I say, "Why did you come to this bar tonight?"

"Katie. She made me promise to stop by and just see where the night went." A hint of something hides in her tone when she speaks.

"Do you regret coming?" I walk around her, eyeing her to watch her reaction.

"I haven't come yet." She's got spirit. I like her wit. "I'll let you know if I regret it later. "

"Tell me, Constance. What do you want me to do to you?" My shoulder is pressed to the front of hers as we face opposite directions. With my lips to her ear, I whisper, "What gets you off?"

Her lips part and I think she's going to speak, but she sucks in a ragged breath instead. Keeping her eyes forward, she releases it.

I place a small, and light kiss just under her earlobe. Her neck is tilted away, opening her up to me. I ask, "What is your pleasure?"

"I'm not sure."

"You don't know what you like?"

She licks her lips, then as if she's confessing a dark secret, replies, "I know what feels good."

"Tell me what makes you feel good, Constance."

"Being touched."

Placing my hand on her thigh, I tease her. "Like that? Does that feel good?"

Her small smile kills me in the best of ways. "It does, but—"

"But what?" I kiss her neck again, and then slide the bridge of my nose against her, taking in a deep breath. Rich vanilla coats her skin. She's absolutely edible. Her shyness is an aphrodisiac. My cock reacting—hard, a throb buried within building. I move my hand higher and when I cup her pussy I hear the soft hitch in her breathing.

"That. I want to be touched there."

"Touched or licked or eaten? Tell me exactly what you want, baby."

Her lids flutter closed and she leans back opening like a flower for me. "I want your hands on me."

"My hand is on you," I challenge, wanting her to say it. "Vocalize it. Own it. Give into that carnal side I know lies just beneath this fancy suit you wear as armor everyday." I scrape my teeth across the base of her neck while I rub gently between her legs. "Here, between these walls, with me, you can drop your shield."

"In me." Like a flurry from the sky, the words fall from her lips, "In me. Deep inside me. I want you to make me come."

The right side of my mouth quirks up. "You're so fucking sexy, Constance." My fingers are deft, her belt opened, the pants unbuttoned, and the zipper down.

She watches the frenzy, keeping her eyes focused below her waist. "Go slow. It's been a while."

My hands stall. When I look up, a contradiction is laden in her eyes. Innocence comingles in the brightest greens, which is so unexpected from a woman who wears a power suit. "How long?"

The pink that highlights her cheeks isn't from shyness this time, but embarrassment. I hate it on her.

"You have nothing to be ashamed of."

"Is everyone you're with . . ." She looks around while building her courage. When her gaze returns to mine, she finishes, "Experienced?"

Yes. "No," I lie so she doesn't wither before me. She's so beautiful when she's blooming. Taking each word into careful consideration and using her chosen one, I ask, "Are you *experienced*?"

"Not fully," she confesses.

Narrowing my eyes at her, I probe, "Not fully as innnnn . . ."

Her voice is so quiet I barely hear her when she says, "Not all the way."

Virgin! I try to keep my eyes from bulging. I didn't know there were virgins in New York. She's like a unicorn. A rainbow unicorn that shits Skittles. A myth. An urban legend. Damn. She's a virgin. *Just Wow.* I want to ask how she held onto that V card for this long, but at the same time, I'm so fucking turned on that she seems to trust me with it that I'm left perplexed over how this night should go. There's no way I'm bending her over like this is just any other night. It's not for her, and I'm starting to think it's not for me either. "So maybe we don't have sex." As she swallows my words, I zip her pants back up, and she buttons them closed while looking disappointed. I ask, "Do you like to dance?"

"Yes."

There's that pretty girl again. Knowing I've put her at ease, I rub the back of my fingers over her cheek. "Let's start there then."

"Okay."

I pull my phone from my pocket and flip through my playlists. *Seduction* is too sultry. *Hard Fuck* is too, well, hard. Lots of Nine Inch Nails on that playlist. Scrolling down, I find my *Take Your Time* playlist. This is actually one I listen to when I'm at home and trying to wind down after a long shift. I've never played it for a woman. It makes me feel unsteady, but she opened up to me, so I feel safe to share a private side of myself with her.

The first song starts playing through the speaker on the filing cabinet and her smile grows. "I love this song," she says much more at ease, her shoulders relaxing.

Taking her hand in mine, I put my other on her hip and slide it up to her waist. "Dance with me, Constance." Our bodies are flush, her breasts rising and falling against my chest. When we start to sway, her breathing picks up. I press my cheek to her temple and we move together. I close my eyes and get lost in the feel of her and the music. Our breath is the only sound between us. Our hearts beat, the thump felt hard in my chest. "You're so beautiful."

She leans farther into me. Reaching up, I pull the silver clip that's holding her perfectly in place hair, and toss it onto the desk. Her hair comes tumbling down over her shoulders burying my nose in her soft locks. I stay, not wanting to move away.

Intimacy is not my specialty. It's not something I crave or need. I have a good life. I'm happy. A successful business. I have great friends and I'm close to my family. But this feels good. Being this close to her, feeling her nerves soften her edges as she molds to me—I like this. Maybe too much.

Chapter Three

Vanilla is now my all time favorite scent, dark brunette with a heavy dose of midnight mixed in, and a pink that reminds me of a rosé wine I discovered at a winery in Sonoma last summer. Constance —my new favorite name.

I know she can feel how hard my body is, and I'm not referring to the ab or bicep muscles I've worked hard to achieve. She's polite enough not to say anything, and if I'm not mistaken, she might have moved closer. Constance might have a naughty side after all. I can't resist her any longer. I kiss the back of her jaw and she bends away, giving me more access. My tongue traces the outline and I press my lips to her skin again, this time gently sucking. I whisper, "How do you feel about kissing?"

"I like," she starts, then clears her throat. "I like kissing."

"Good because I really want to kiss you right now." I take possession of her lips just as she opens her mouth to speak again. Her heated breath coats my tongue as it peeks out to run along the inside of her upper lip.

The sweetest of little moans drifts from her lips when we part. Her eyes remain closed, a small smile on her mouth, and a satisfied release of breath is heard. I kiss the corner of her mouth and whisper, "Open your eyes, beautiful."

When she does, the smile is still there. "You're a very good kisser."

Holding hands with her, I reply, "So are you." I chuckle looking down and rub my thumb over my bottom lip. Biting it, I look up, now suddenly feeling shy—so unlike me that I take a moment to take her in. What is it about her that has me off my game? I shake my head just enough to shake some sense into myself. "I want to kiss you again."

"Why does it sound like a question?"

"Because if I do, I might not stop with a kiss."

"Then don't stop with a kiss."

Back in the game, I run my fingers into her hair and grip the back of her head. "Oh baby, you don't even know what you've done."

"Tell me."

"How about I show you instead?"

One nod. Instant permission to make her feel so good she won't stop thinking about this night for months. Our mouths crash together and our tongues begin to embrace each other. With her hands on my waist, I take them and slide them over my chest and around my neck. "Hold onto me."

As soon as I feel her hold on me tighten, I spin her to the side and move her quickly back against the wall with the dry erase board. Her hair messes up the tally the guys and I had going, but I don't give a damn. She tastes too good and feels even better.

Another moan rushes out and she squirms against me.

My cock begins straining against my jeans. She might be the hardest fucking thing I've ever tempted, tortured, or teased myself with. Goddamn it. I pop the button of her pants and my hand is dipping below the waistband before the zipper is down. "So good, baby. I'm going to make you come all over my hand and scream the lord's name while doing it."

Her body moves in fluid waves against me, against my hand, begging me to take her. "Hardy," comes out as a curse and a blessing.

Flicking sweet afflictions, I ravage her neck with my mouth. "So fucking sexy. Say it again."

This time it's even breathier. "Hardy."

I give her what her body craves and ride my fingers though her slickness, parting her. She's wet, warm, so fucking free with me and that's all it takes for my throbbing to amp up another level. I press against her to find some relief. My dick is a fucking torpedo impeded by denim. *Fuck.* I don't know how I'm going to survive this encounter if I can't sink deep into her tight heat.

A virgin, I remind myself. She deserves more than hair used as an eraser and a wall fuck for her first time. A virgin. I didn't see that one coming . . . coming, yes, but not coming. She ordered that Gimlet like a seasoned pro. Maybe I'm getting sick and my sex-dar is off.

"Hardy, I want you."

My name pulls me back to the moment and I adjust my hand. "I should go slow," I reply more for myself than her.

She lifts higher on her toes and pushes her pants open for me. "No. Faster. You can touch me. I'm not delicate. I won't break."

"I'm not worried about breaking you, sweetheart. I'm worried about the excruciatingly rock hard woody I'll be sporting the rest of the night."

A devilish grin appears and she says, "Then let me help you."

I'm not one to say no to a generous offer and it damn well beats me beating off later to the memories of how her mouth forms this little "O" just below the bow of her upper lip.

My jeans are unbuttoned, my fly unzipped, my cock freed. "Holy—" She gasps.

Normally when a woman gasps, I'd worry, but I get this a lot when Big Richard comes out to play. With a twitch, he greets her, practically jumping into her hand. Do it. Grab me, he entices. *Bad boy.*

Her hand wraps around me and she slides up to the tip and back down. "Your hand feels so good wrapped around my cock." When her eyes lift to look into mine, I put my lips to her ear, and whisper, "I can't wait to have more of you around me." And there's that little hitch I wanted to hear. "Not tonight, but soon. You'll come back and see me." What the fuck? Did I just talk about the future with a woman? Wonder if I have a fever?

I get back to the business at hand, the business of making her come. Moving my hand deeper between her delicate folds, I tease her entrance. Her hand on me tightens —*Bingo.* One finger sinks deep inside, her warm walls engulfing. "Holy Jack fucking Daniels."

Her lips are against my jaw, her breath coming out in quick pants. Her grip around my neck brings her closer to me and I can't wait. I have no fucking patience when it comes to her and the way she wiggles against me. I push another finger in slowly, and lean back to watch her. The back of her throat is revealed and my mind is spinning.

I'm going to explode soon. This woman is driving me nuts with how good this feels and we're only making out.

Like two teenagers. My core starts to wind, tightening under her ministrations. With my thumb, I find her clit and she bucks forward. One touch and she's that sensitive. God, I might be falling in love. What the fuck is wrong with me?

Shit. Big Richard bucks on his own accord. "Damn, baby. I'm close." Now I'm the one that sounds all breathy. The coil gets even tighter. I'm about to spring to life, but I've got to get her off first. Thrusting gently, I start to fuck her with my fingers, my hips are pressed against her, trapping our hands between us. I have no fucking self-control. This is insane. Insanely amazing.

Our hands are in sync, our bodies begging for release, and then the back of her head hits the board behind her and my name comes tripping from her lips right after God and sandwiched between an orgasm that sets mine in motion.

"Fuck. Oh baby. Yes, Constance. Fuck. Yes." Ribbons spurt, covering my stomach and my shirt as I vanish into the bright lights of the dark blissful abyss.

When I open my eyes, hers open just as languidly. The pink that I could become so easily accustomed to has spread to her neck and collarbone and the tips of her ears. I tuck myself back in and with my free hand, touch her cheek, and lean my forehead against hers. "You're stunning."

She smiles and a soft laugh tickles my mouth. I part my lips wanting more, wanting to inhale her deep inside. Slowly, I slide my hand free and she releases me. Looking down, she laughs again, a little louder this time. "We're a mess."

"A beautiful mess."

"I bet you say that to all the girls."

My smile slips away. "I don't."

She reads me well. "I didn't mean you really say that to all the girls you're with."

I settle the panic in her eyes, preferring the after-orgasm look instead. "It's okay. Just don't think I'm like this with everyone because I'm not."

The smile lines ease and her expression lightens. "Why are you so sweet to me? Even after I told you Katie O'Dowd sent me to see you?"

"Because you're nothing like Katie O'Dowd."

"How am I different?" she asks, just a whisper as we still hold each other.

"She came here looking for a good time and that's all she was. But you," I say, tucking some hair behind her ear, "I'll remember long after tonight." I kiss her sweetly, which seems to be the only way to kiss someone as pretty as her when she's looking at me like I just hung the moon for her.

Zipping her pants and fastening her belt, her shyness returns slowly, the blush disappearing from her chest and centering on her cheeks. She looks down, and asks, "Why?"

"Because you think you came here for sex when you were really just looking for a connection."

Her green eyes look like jade in the dim lights of the office, her beautiful innocence shining through. "I've done this sort of thing before." She tries to sound bold, but I see through the act.

"Have you now?"

"I'm not such a Goody Two-shoes." She raises her chin, trying to build some offense to the smile on my face that makes it clear I don't believe her.

"You're not a Gimlet girl. Why'd you order it?"

"Because I wanted to be one, someone who orders what they want and owns it, someone who owns who they are without apologies."

"You are that woman. You just don't know it yet." I bend and kiss her on the neck, just because I want to keep kissing her, touching her, keep her here longer than my break allows. On the other side of the office door the music and crowd have gotten louder. I glance toward the door. The bar should be in full swing by now and I'm probably needed, but Constance makes me want to stay.

"I got stood up by a guy, but please don't take pity on me."

"There's no pity when I look at you. Only beauty."

She sighs, and touches my cheek. "Look, you're really great, but I've taken enough of your time. I should let you get back."

"He's an asshole and you deserve better than you realize." This time I kiss her on the lips, full on, tongues mingling. My heart beats harder and my body leans in, the warning signs red-flagging themselves—*Don't get too close.* When our lips part, I whisper, "I don't want to go back to work, but I need to."

She smiles, her arms lax as she lets them hang around my neck. "Come on. Don't want to get that boss mad at you."

"Yup, I heard he's an asshole too."

"He's not, but I think he likes to pretend he is." She lifts up and kisses my cheek. "I'm going to use the restroom. I'm kind of a mess. Then I'll see you out there?"

"I'll see you out there."

She lets her hand drag across my chest until she's out of reach. She unlocks the door, and with her hand on the knob, she turns back. "Thank you, Hardy."

I nod, not sure how to reply. Is she thanking me for getting her off? It didn't feel shallow. "Come see me at the bar when you're done."

"Okay." She walks out and shuts the door behind her.

I remain there a few seconds too long, staring at the back of the wood door. There are only two rules:

Rule number one: Don't get too close.

Rule number two: Never fall in love.

Why do I already feel like I broke one rule and I'm about to shatter the second?

Chapter Four

Is it really so bad to want to see Constance again? It's not a crime to actually connect with a woman on a deeper level. Is it?

I rub my chest over these mixed up emotions, hoping to break them up, and send them on their way. I have a good life. I don't need to mess it up like some of the other guys have with marriage, kids, affairs, and divorces. We've seen a few bartenders come through here, each of their stories unique. I could have predicted the ones who'd end up with happy lives and as the saying goes—happy wives.

Some bartenders were smart enough to take their skills, and utilize them in the real world. Hence the happy wives. The others, who screwed up elsewhere came back begging for jobs they lost in the first place. I get it. The attention we get at The Hideaway is addicting. It strokes our egos on a nightly basis. Some are just dumb enough to believe they deserve it, that it will last outside these walls. It doesn't.

And if I'm being honest with myself, which is iffy part of the time and what I try my best to be the other half, I don't even remember how those two rules came to be. I've been in relationships. They just weren't good. I don't have lingering, unresolved feelings. I was fine moving on. What I'm starting to think is that they didn't make me feel at all. I mean if everything's resolved before you walk away, what mark did they leave on your life? None worth remembering.

But here I stand, still staring at a door I've watched close plenty of times, and walked out right after just fine. Yet, looking at that door now, all I wish is that this one time it would open and she would walk right back in.

I walk around the cabinet, reminding myself of the rules and why they exist, grab a pack of wipes and clean myself up. A few shirts hang in the closet from what I picked up from the dry cleaners earlier. I grab a gray one and slip it on, and then bend down to look in a mirror on the wall and fix my hair. When I'm ready, I walk out and down the hall. I push open the door to the main part of the bar. My ears are instantly assaulted by the noise.

Women touch me and call me by my name. I'm treated like a rock star in this bar. I'm friendly, say hi, but keep moving. I lift the panel and step behind the bar. Eddie smirks. He thinks he knows what's up, but really, he doesn't. He doesn't see my heart about to pound out of my chest, or the way I look toward the bathrooms anxious to see her again. He doesn't notice that I bring down the most expensive tequila in the bar and mix up a Paloma for a woman who's not even here. Nope, I smile and pretend I just got laid. Sure, I came, harder than I have in a long time and I wasn't even inside her. But I was with her and that in and of itself, was worth coming over.

I pour two glasses of white wine and make a margarita before Constance makes her way back to me and finds a vacated barstool. I deliver her drink and lean in so she can hear me . . . Fine, I pretend that's why I lean in. I just like being near her. "It's a Paloma. I like it with salt shaken in, but I'll leave that for you to decide." I set the saltshaker down in front of her.

"Why did you make me a Paloma?"

"When this drink is made right it's delicate on the palate." I take my fingers and suck the tips into my mouth. Her eyes are glued on my mouth, her lips parted, and her breath picks up when I pull my fingers slowly back out. "The grapefruit with the club soda balances the liquor. It's sophisticated, but refreshing, like you."

"Thank you," she replies.

"You're welcome." A lady with a strong east coast accent calls my name. I recognize it instantly. I've never slept with her, but that's not due to her lack of trying. Before I go, I add, "By the way, your hair looks beautiful down. You should wear it like that more often."

"Maybe I will." Her smile is wide and relaxed. She takes a sip of her drink.

I wink and walk to serve the other lady, but keep my eye on Constance. That's when it happens. Giant hairy mitts for hands hide her eyes when someone comes up behind her. When she turns, her eyes go wide, obviously recognizing this douche. She's okay, so I help Mitzi, from the Upper East Side. If her friends only knew how she trolled Brooklyn for hookups she might not be so easily accepted on the social scene of Manhattan.

While blending Mitzi's favorite drink, a banana daiquiri, I glance down Constance's way. She steals a glimpse of me before the asshole snaps his fingers to bring her attention back to him.

Asshole.

Ohhhh. Is that the asshole that stood her up tonight?

I serve Mitzi and another woman vying for my attention, then check on Constance. Standing right in front of her, I rest my hands on the bar. "Everything okay down here?"

The asshole flashes a fifty, and replies, "I need a hoppy IPA, and the lady needs another."

Figures. IPA's are generally bitter, similar to the taste he's left in my mouth. I look to her and sadness has crept up on her, a lot like this guy. She pushes her empty glass away, and mouths, "I'm sorry," but says, "I'm good, Hardy. Thanks."

Asshole says, "Hardy, be a good barkeep and run along and get me that beer. Seems I'm drinking alone."

Ignoring him, I stay focused on Constance. "Hey?"

"Yeah?" she replies quietly.

"I can throw him out if you want."

That makes her laugh and it was worth being belittled by him to hear that effervescent sound. "I'm good."

"Well, just let me know. I know a guy."

"The boss."

"Yep. The boss." I leave her to go get that bitter beer for the asshole. When I set it down, as much as I want to spend time with her, I don't waste time and hang around with him there. My bar is packed and three people deep down the length of it. I get to cocktailing.

I find time to drop off a fresh drink for her and then another. I start to think I might have to cut her off soon. The asshole is taking her laughter and smile as an open invitation and crowding her. She's nice enough not to complain, but it pisses me the fuck off.

It's getting close to midnight and she looks tired. I know I am, but I have another hour before I get off work. When the asshole snaps his fingers at me three times, I go begrudgingly. "Close my tab."

A please would be nice, but what the fuck ever with him. It has started to feel like Constance is avoiding eye contact with me, so my mood has soured.

~~Rule number one: Don't get too close.~~

Fucked that one right up. Now I'm left with the remnants to clean up. At least rule number two is safe. I hand him his change and just as I'm about to tell Constance that it was a pleasure to not just meet her, but spend time with her, she turns to the woman next to her, and says, "The Gimlets are amazing. You should order one from Hardy, in particular." She's nodding and though I can tell she's definitely tipsy, she didn't seem drunk until now. "He loves serving Gimlets. Don't you, Hardy?"

Confused to where she's going with this, I eye her, and whisper, "What are you doing?"

"Helping."

"Helping how exactly?"

"Helping you find your next one." Staring at her, I watch her nod, signaling to her barstool neighbor. "You know, a Gimlet girl."

"Don't," I reply, flatly. "Don't help. I'm not a gigolo."

"Oh, I didn't mean to imply that."

"What did you mean then?"

Asshole leans over. "Hey buddy, I don't know what's going on here, but it needs to end. She's with me, so stop hitting on the customers, and stick with what you do best— serving them."

My spine straightens and my fists itch to punch his fucking face for talking to me like that. "I think it's time for you to leave."

"I'm a good paying customer. Don't make me report you to the manager."

"Hardy's Hideaway. I own this place, so get the fuck out and don't come back."

Looking at Constance, he says, "Come on. It's late and I have a deposition in the morning."

Constance's eyes close. When she reopens them, a muted shame is seen in the usually rich color, dulling them. "Hardy," she starts, but asshole yanks her barstool back and paws her hand. Before she's pulled away, she says, "I'll see you." What she said earlier slips out without the most important word attached—again—and I hate that I notice.

Instead of watching her leave, I push down the sickening feeling in my stomach and start serving customers again. But that damn feeling doesn't ease up once they're gone and I stop, and look up. *Gone.*

I'm just not ready to have her gone—from the bar . . . *from my life?* I toss the ice scoop into the bin and hightail it out from behind the bar and weave through the crowd toward the exit. Pushing the door open, it's cold and snowing and I don't have a jacket on, but step out anyway. She's twenty or so feet away waiting for a cab. "Constance," I call, just before she heads to the cab asshole has hailed.

Her eyes go wide when she sees me, and says something to her date before coming back to me. "What are you doing out here?"

I'm dumbfounded by the way she's acting. Is it a show she's putting on for that asshole? Or is this the real her? "I'm not chained behind the bar."

"You're twisting my words." She looks nervous, and glances back at her date before turning back to me. "What did you want to say?"

"You know what's funny?"

"What?"

"I've hooked up with more than my share of women in

my life. I never felt ashamed or apologetic about it because I respected them. I gave them a good time. I had a good time, and it was always an act between two consenting adults."

Her date holds the cab door open. Impatiently, he says, "Come on, Virginia. It's cold."

Virginia. Time is ticking, the seconds going from one beat to three in the blink of an eye. "I've owned every encounter I've had and never felt cheap. Until tonight, *Constance.*" I back toward the door, grabbing the handle.

Those eyelids I enjoyed kissing an hour earlier close tightly. When she opens them, she says, "I'm sor—"

I don't want to hear it, so I open the door and cut her off, "And for the record, I wouldn't have kept you waiting even a second knowing some other guy could come along and steal you away. Much less stand you up."

"Hardy?"

"Goodbye."

I wish I could leave and go home. I'm not in the mood to stay, which is a first for me. I love my job, but disappointment is settling into my bones, an unfamiliar feeling of wishing it could have been different with her. I'm not sure what to make of my emotions. They've never flip-flopped on me like this. I'm probably just tired.

The door closes behind me, and the crowd inside welcomes me with a cheer. With rule number two safely intact, it's time to celebrate that same victory, though it doesn't feel like one deep down. "Eddie, a shot for everyone."

Chapter Five

My head is pounding. I drank way too much last night. I don't normally drink on a Monday or while I'm working long shifts, but I needed something to wash away . . . I shake my head irritated with myself for even thinking twice about Constance much less thinking about her the minute I wake up.

Women don't affect me. Not usually. But there's something about her, something different that made me want to spend time with her, still kind of do. *Fuck.* I enjoy a good morning tug, but she's got Big Richard all screwed up. If I didn't know better, I'd think he's all fucked up over her too. My annoyance with his floppy behavior is unsettling on many levels.

I reach over and pop some Ibuprofen, then down a bottle of water from my nightstand. Lying on my back, I stare up at the ceiling. It's still dark out. If I can get my ass out of bed, I can run the bridge while the sun is rising.

Motivation is key when it comes to me. Watching the sunrise while on the Brooklyn Bridge is something I like to do at least once a week. One reason is there's nobody on the pedestrian path at that time of day. Another, I get to laugh at the poor saps commuting into Manhattan. I'm so glad I don't have to report to an eight-to-five five days a week. I did that for years and I never want to do it again. Seeing the suits stuck in their cars and cabs reminds me of how good I have it.

Motivation, my friend. *Mot-i-vation*.

I flip the covers off and head to the bathroom. After shaking the snake, I pull on a pair of tighter than a duck's ass compression pants and then loose athletic pants. I'm not letting anyone see me in tights, but they keep me warm, so two layers it is.

Three layers on the upper body, gloves, thick socks, sneakers, and a hat and I'm out the door running. My headache has subsided and pounding the pavement beats my head pounding. My breath comes out in puffs of white air as I work my way through the neighborhood and up toward the bridge. It's a sea of red brake lights on my approach. I smirk, feeling mighty proud that I'm choosing to be awake at this hour instead of forced to be. There's a difference, and I worked hard to have the option.

Pumping my arms, the slow incline becomes easier as I pick up speed. I see my stopping point ahead and run faster. I hit my mark and stop, bent over, out of breath. When I look up at the Manhattan skyline, I'm in awe of the way the sun rises giving the world a golden hue, even if just for a moment in time. If the run hadn't, the sunrise would have taken my breath away.

My heart rate evens and I stand there at the mercy of its beauty. Forget last night and troubles that aren't really troubles. Look at the hope that rises in the east and sets in the west. Today is a new day, wiping our slates clean again.

I start to get cold standing there, so I continue jogging

the rest of the bridge enjoying the view with the slower pace. I cut right, heading for the Manhattan Bridge to loop back to Brooklyn. Stopped at a light, I push the button impatiently ready to carry on with my run and get back.

"Hardy?"

I swear I heard my name. Looking over my shoulder, nope. No one there.

"Hardy?" Glancing over my other shoulder there's a yellow cab. The passenger window is up and the cab driver looks half asleep. My gaze follows further back. Looking too beautiful for hers or my own good, I smile just from seeing her. *Constance.* Shit. It's not Constance. I forgot. It's Virginia. "Hi," she says as if I've just made her day.

I'm still smiling like a loon when I realize I'm supposed to be mad at her. "Hey," I reply, checking to make sure the light hasn't changed. That sinking feeling from last night sits solidly in the gut of my stomach. "You live in Brooklyn?" I ask, making casual conversation since we're both stuck awkwardly at the same light. "I figured you for a Manhattanite."

"I am." Her expression falls, reading mine. "I know you don't want to hear it, but I'm sorry."

"No need," I reply, waving the apology away so I don't have to accept it. The pedestrian signal gives me the go-ahead, so go ahead I do. "Have a good life."

"Bye," I hear behind me as I jog forward.

Here's the problem with the city—too many damn lights. Not twenty-five yards later and we're both stuck at a light right next to each other again. When I spy her cab next to me, I start debating: should I say hi again or pretend I don't see her?

"Hi again," she says.

"Hi," I acknowledge her against my better judgment,

but I hate being rude even if we're only meant to be a one-time kind of thing. Besides mucking up my morning wood earlier, now she's screwing with my body *and* mind. I look down and see my pants pushing out. My jog is supposed to center me. I usually have clarity and solid focus afterwards, but when I look down, I'm solid all right.

I'm actually impressed with the strength of these compression pants. They're doing a fair job of restraining the will of a thousand armies down there. I'm still cautious about looking at her directly. She has some kind of super power that makes me want to toss my heart right into the ring of fire. And I'm not talking about anal, though I'm not opposed to that, quite the opposite. *Fuck.*

She interrupts my pity party. "It's good to see you again."

I pack away my tiny imaginary violin, and rub the back of my neck. "You mean from the last block?"

"No, from last night."

"Yeah, okay." I'm not sure what else to say to that. The woman vexes me. First off, how does someone who looks like her stay a virgin? Secondly, is she still a virgin after last night or did she give it up to that asshole after I warmed her up? Fucking asshole. I start running because the street is clear of traffic and I don't know what to say to her. Does she want me to make her feel better? Tell her it's okay that she made me feel used and slightly dirty, though the dirty part in reference to good or bad is still up for debate?

The cars start moving just as I reach the next intersection. In my peripheral I see the bright yellow cab slowly pulling up to the light. "For fuck's sake. What the fuck?"

The cabbie's passenger window rolls down and he leans down so I can see him. "Hey, mister, this could be a lot less weird if you hear the lady out."

The back window rolls down and Constance *Virginia* looks mortified. The problem is she looks so damn good, even in mortification, that I walk up to the cab and open the door. "Scoot over." After I slide in next to her, I shut the door, and ask, "Where are we headed?"

The driver replies in a crotchety voice, "Financial District."

Oh, now *he's* bothered. The irony is not missed. Turning toward her, I ask, "Why?"

The cab starts moving again, and Con—Virginia answers, "Because I'll be late to work if we don't."

"You work in the Financial District?"

"Yes."

"What do you do?"

"I'm a financial analyst."

"I swore off that industry when I left Manhattan three years ago."

"What do you mean you swore it off?"

"Why did you lie about your name?"

"I don't know. I just wanted to be someone else for the night."

"Why?"

"The truth is I was ashamed to be doing what I was doing."

"What were you doing?"

"I wanted to feel good. I wanted to know what it feels like. Katie says I'm beautiful. I think I am, but something's broken because I can't seem to find love."

"With a stranger? As for love, you weren't looking for love, sweetheart. You were looking for a good time. I get it. I really do, but that's not how your first time should go down." My gaze dips down her body, that feeling in my gut returns. I can't believe I didn't notice sooner. "Considering you're wearing the same clothes as last night, guess you found it anyway."

The cab comes to a stop and as much as I want to know why she's shame-cabbing it back into the city. The stop is my cue. I open the door and get out. Just as she's about to speak, I say, "Have a good life, Virginia." I shut the door and start running again. With the Manhattan Bridge up ahead, I pick up speed not wanting to get trapped at a light again. When I make a right, back on track, I'm tempted to look back, but I know there's no point. She slept with that asshole after spending time with me. There's nothing really to discuss anymore.

When I turn down my street, I go inside the coffee shop. The morning line is long, but I wait. Watching people is a good way to take my mind off things. My favorite barista is working today. When I reach the counter, she eyes me over the pastry display. "Good morning, Hardy."

"Good morning, Luisa."

She giggles as her smile grows. "What can I get you this morning?"

"The usual."

With a tease in her tone, she says, "Coming right up."

Not able to stop my mind going to the gutter, I reply, "You're naughty this morning, but I'm naughtier at night." I wink.

"I remember all too well, Hardy."

"When are you going to stop in The Hideaway again?"

She raises her hand and wiggles her finger. "No more Hideaway for me. The boyfriend has become the fiancé."

"Whoa," I say, thrilled for her. "That's fantastic news. Congratulations."

"Thank you. Just happened over the weekend, so it's new." She shrugs to play it off.

"I'm happy for you, Luisa. You deserve good things."

That brightens her back up. She hands me my coffee—simple, classic, black—and leans in. "You do too, Hardy. Don't settle for anything less." Speaking in her usual chipper voice, she says, "Coffee's on me. Have a great Tuesday."

"Thanks. See you soon." I start walking, but say, "Congrats again. He's a lucky guy."

"Yes, he is." She laughs and I leave feeling a little lighter myself.

The street has gotten more crowded with the rush to work happening all around me. Two blocks down, I punch in the code for my building and head up the two flights to my second-floor walk up. I toss my keys in the silver bowl my mom sent me from Europe last year for Christmas. I kick the door closed and bolt it. My sneakers are toed off just inside the door, my socks pulled off and left in the hall as I start for the bathroom. I set my coffee on the kitchen bar as I pass. My three shirts are pulled off as one and dropped just inside my bedroom. I start the shower and peel my pants off waiting for the water to warm.

I rest my palms to the cold marble and check my complexion. It's clear with a healthy sheen of sweat earned from my run. Running my hands through my hair, I look back at my reflection and for the first time in years, I wonder if this is it. Is this how life is always going to be? Simple and uncomplicated, like my coffee? I glare at myself. Thoughts like this haven't crossed my mind since I was working seventy to eighty hours a week in the city. Thoughts like this are the reason I cashed out financially and left a career I thought I liked. I didn't. It was making me into a person I didn't want to be, a person I didn't like, but didn't realize it until I woke up between two women who were traders down on Wall Street in an apartment in SoHo that belonged to my boss.

My boss was found under the nanny by his wife when she came home from visiting her dying mother with their two kids. The divorce papers cited cocaine and philandering and listed me as a liability. My hands were clean when it came to the drugs, as for the philandering—I didn't make him do it. But I didn't stop him either.

I resigned that day and I found a new job. He went on to marry his secretary and had another kid within the next year. After I heard about his first wife's large settlement, I figured she was off living the high life without the baggage of her cheating ex-husband. Then I ran into his wife in Saks Fifth Avenue three years ago. She was on the phone arguing. I heard her tell the other person that her kids missed him and that they hadn't seen him since his "new" family was complete with the little boy he always wanted. She hung up on him and broke down crying.

I approach with caution, with care. She looks tired, not like the woman I knew years earlier on the arm of my boss. Everything I had seen was one-sided, his side. Now staring at the other side, I felt like shit. I was part of this. I helped cause this. Sure there was a huge group of us always partying together, living the high life as we raked in the money. But there were consequences I never had to face. I was single. I only had to think of myself, and that's all I had done. Until that moment. Seeing her break down after losing her husband, her kids losing their dad, and that love for money is no substitute for the real thing, I walk up to her, and say, "I'm sorry."

She looks up. The beautiful woman that was once the star of the holiday parties now carried dark circles under her eyes and her wounds in the blues. As her eyes look into mine,

I wait for her to speak, for her forgiveness, for anything. I don't get her words. I get slapped across the face, and left with words that scar me to this day. "Don't ever fall in love, Hardy." She walked away that day, I hope feeling a little lighter.

I walked away from Manhattan. I walked away from the girls who I was dating because they fit an image I was trying to uphold, but had no depth. I walked away from my parent's pride in my accomplishments and took on their worry that I would be homeless. They didn't realize the size of my bank account, the money I'd earned off the hard work of others while I bet theirs on the stock market. It had paid off. It was legal, but certain investments made me feel dirty. The clients were thrilled with their profits, but I only felt a sense of loss. That was when I left the life I'd been living behind, donated what I call my dirty wealth to charities that my mom helped me find. I took everything else and put it into the bar to start over. I sold my apartment with the great view in a trendy part of the city for millions and invested the rest. My financial advisor says I'm set for life.

As I step into the shower, I drench my hair and let the water run down my body. I spent three years living a life that destroyed my insides. I've spent the last three building a life that's good, feels clean, and honorable. So I have sex with some of the ladies—no harm done if it's between two adults who understand the rules.

Virginia has me feeling reflective for some reason. I'm not worried about her. Rule number two is intact for all time. If I learned anything from my boss's ex-wife, it was don't ever fall in love. I don't need the baggage of relationships. Life should be simple, easy, uncomplicated.

The problem I'm now faced with is if I really believe life should be that easy, that uncomplicated, and that simple, then why am I still thinking about a girl I met on a random Monday at the bar? A girl who was never a Gimlet and always a Paloma. Yep, I called it all wrong last night and I'm starting to wonder if my heart is the one that will pay the price.

Chapter Six

When I reach for the door, I notice there's a smudge on the gold lettering of Hardy. I rub my elbow over it using the soft material of my coat to make it shine again. "There. Much better." Yeah, yeah, I talk to myself sometimes. Whatever. I'm damn proud of this bar and that my name's the one on that smudgy door.

When I walk inside, the happy hour crowd is in full swing, every table occupied. I stop by the far end of the bar when I see Clive. "How's it going?"

His smile grows. I've seen that one before. He's either just gotten laid or about to hone in on his prey. "Picking up." Despite the old man name, he's one of my biggest earners. The ladies love him. I'm six two. He's twenty-five and built like a beast at six five.

"Business or you?"

"Ha! You know me well. Little honey-colored sweet bee over by the dartboard."

I look behind me. A pretty woman with a sincere laugh

is pulling a dart out of the wall. He always did like the doe-eyed blondes. "Twenty-one?"

"Don't worry. I carded. Twenty-three last week."

Nodding my approval, I reply, "Good." Pushing off the bar, I head to the back. "Eddie will be here soon, but you know where to find me if you need anything."

"You working behind the bar tonight, boss?"

"Trying to catch up on the books for last week."

"We've got the front covered."

"I have no doubt." I greet a few ladies on the way back. The hall is quiet, my office quieter when I unlock the door. The dry erase board is the first thing I see when I enter—smeared ink where Const—Virginia's hair rubbed against it when I rubbed against her. Damn, she was beautiful with her lips parted, her breath becoming mine, and her pussy vibrating around my fingers.

That same memory inspired me to get off another time in the shower this morning. I should be mad at her, offended she treated our time together less than respectful like I had. But I didn't just have a good time with her; I had a good time getting to know her. It would have been nice to have more time with her. Asshole put an end to that. He had some nerve showing up to collect her like he owns her. And what the fuck? Was she drunk enough to fall right into his hands after I warmed her up? I sit down at my desk and switch on the lamp. I need to bury myself in some numbers instead of burying my thoughts into her deep heat.

Rubbing my eyes, I glance at my watch. Two hours. The nightly transition has happened and the night crowd is growing. My mind drifts. I hate unsettled feelings and that's what I have from last night. And this morning. She was a virgin and yet, she went home with him and what? Banged him. I don't regret not having sex with her. It goes back to respect—I respect her so it's hard to hate her. We all make mistakes. So maybe if she comes around again I'll give her another chance.

I doubt she will, but it helps to ease the little bit of guilt I've carried over from bailing from that cab this morning. Now that I'm caught up with last week's inventory and balanced the books, I stand, looking in the mirror behind the desk and straighten my tie. I don't have a uniform here, but the guys tend to dress nicer. Keeps the clientele happy and helps project a more upscale ambiance. Yeah, yeah, we hook up sometimes, but we're single, so it's all-good.

I turn out the lamp and leave the office. Making my way through the tables and full bar reminds me again of how fortunate I am. I worked for this, gave up my past life in hopes of something better. The hours are long, but so were the hours at my last job. At least this one comes with perks.

"Hi, Hardy."

Seeing one of my favorite margarita drinkers, I stop and swing around the back of her chair to kiss her on the cheek. "Hi Margot. Good to see you."

"Better seeing you. Now give me a spin and let me get the full view."

I'm tempted. She's good in bed. She's also married. Now. I'll clarify that she wasn't when we hooked up last year. Her being married means she's off-limits now. I may live by two rules, but I make the guys adhere to that one. The last thing I need or the bar needs is an angry husband out for revenge. Anyway, ever since I ran into my ex-boss's ex-wife, I keep things in my life less muddied. I kiss Margot on the cheek and make sure she's good with her current drink before checking in with Eddie and Clive.

Just five feet from the bar, I stop. I know that midnight hair, lean legs, and another damn suit that does nothing to flatter her figure. Oh wait, maybe I do approve of the suits. Clive gives me a look along with a little head nod toward Virginia.

I feel the tension in my jaw as I walk around the bar. When I see what she's drinking, it lifts just a little. She looks up and gives me an uneasy smile that looks out of place on her. I'm not all bad. I head down to break the pressure before it builds. Her glass has just gone empty and she pushes it forward. Standing in front of her, I ask, "Would you like another Paloma?"

"Are you making it?"

"Making and Shaking."

Even I know how lame that line is, but she laughs. "Then I'll take two."

"Let's start slow."

"I was thinking over."

Working on her drink, my gaze lifts to her. "I recognize you."

Her eyes go wide. "Well, I hope so after what we did."

I chuckle. "I mean this is the woman who caught my attention last night. Bold, empowered, ordering Gimlets as if she actually likes them."

"I do like them," she protests, sitting up straighter.

"Because I make a damn good Gimlet."

"Yes, you do, but what do you mean you recognize me."

I set the glass and a saltshaker in front of her and lean in closer so only she hears. "You're tough, quick wit, and if I'm being honest, which for some reason I am with you, you're the most beautiful woman in here." I take a step back, wanting to leave room for my emotional outpour. I'd wipe it up if I could and reach for a rag out of habit. It's too late. She's enchanted. I've seen that look before. Now I've gone and done it. I bet it was the honesty.

"Why are you telling me this?"

"This woman sitting at my bar right now and that shy girl from last night, they're two different people."

"Which do you prefer?"

"I think you know." I take a step back, not wanting to argue. This is leading into dragging those unresolved feelings up to the surface and I'm not ready to confront those demons.

"I'm sorry, Hardy. I meant what I said this morning and when I say it now." She looks to her barstool neighbors on either side of her and then turns back to me. "What we did and how you treated me—it was beyond what I could have asked of anyone. I didn't deserve you in the first place, but I definitely didn't mean to dismiss you. I'm truly sorry. I hope you can forgive me."

I sigh, already knowing I'll accept. "I'm a sucker for an apology."

"Katie O'Dowd said you might be a suck—"

Pressing my fingers to her mouth before she says anything more, I cut her off and tease, "You need to stop listening to Katie O'Dowd. She talks too much."

"She had a lot of good things to say about you."

"If she has such fond memories, what made her send you in while she stayed home?"

"Pregnant."

Taken aback. I did not see that coming. "I'm not gonna lie. My heart stopped there for a second."

She bursts out laughing. "Don't worry, you're safe. She's only three months along and she's pretty sure it's her husbands."

I start laughing. "Pretty sure?"

"I was joking. "She's happily pregnant *by* her husband."

Not worried in the least, but it's fun to pretend. I wipe

the sweat from my forehead and puff out my cheeks in an exaggerated exhale. "We should drink to that."

"Can you join me?"

"Maybe."

"What will turn that maybe into a yes?"

"Answers."

"I'll give you any answers you want."

I pour a whiskey—neat—and say, "Come on. There's a table over there. We can talk." When I come out from behind the bar, I follow her to the table. Even in that damn suit her jacket is just short enough to show off that great ass. She takes a seat and I sit across from her. "To Katie O'Dowd." I tap my glass to the wood top once, then take a long drink of my whiskey while taking a good look at her. When I set it down, I see how bundled and uptight she seems. She offered, so I'm going to ask the questions. "What's your last name, Virginia?" The name is starting to fit the woman in front of me, feeling more natural to say.

"Ryan. My last name is Ryan."

Virginia Ryan. I like her name, almost as much as I like her. Sure I'm still a little mad at her, but that's just my stubborn side keeping me from a good time. "It's funny we have two first names as our last names."

That keeps that smile, though unsure, hanging on her face long enough for me to memorize her features and see the beauty in her uncertainty. "That is funny. And if we ever got married, I wouldn't have to change my initials."

Normally the reins would be pulled way back at the mere mention of marriage, but when she says it, I find her too cute. "Yep, because stuff like that is important," I tease. As the amusement fades, I get to what I can tell she's antici-pating, maybe dreading. "Why did you leave with that asshole?"

She sighs. Shame covers her when she looks down as if that is the last question she wanted to answer. When her gaze lifts, she takes a deep breath and then exhales. "I don't want to lie to you."

"Then don't."

"I've not told anyone about this, except Katie who called me out on it." I wait, seeing how hard this is for her. I don't want to interrupt since I'm more curious than before. "It may sound naïve . . . I may sound naïve, but I've had a crush on him since the day I started working at the company. He's one of the lawyers there. And I'm completely invisible to him."

"Because he's an asshole."

She laughs. "I guess I'm attracted to assholes." *I'm not an asshole.* "But it is what it is."

"Did you have sex with him?"

A gasp comes out and her eyes are wide. "What? No. Of course not. Why would you think that?"

"Isn't it obvious?" I don't know if my relief can be seen, but I feel it in every cell of my body. Annihilation of rule number one while reloading to take out rule two. Shit. Back up a bit. I need to slow this roll down. "You were wearing the same clothes this morning in the cab that you wore last night and you said you live in Manhattan, but you were driving in from Brooklyn." My replay of her morning appears to entertain her, so much that her laughter echoes around us. The beautiful sound captures an audience from a few nearby tables. "What's so funny?"

"You." Though she's still giggling, she moves in closer, and says, "If I didn't know better, I would say you were jealous."

"Me?" This time I scoff. "To get jealous you have to care and last night was just another night at The Hideaway."

"Wow, way to make a girl feel special."

"You were feeling special. Now that, I will never forget."

"Well my answer is not exciting. I stayed at Katie's. The, as you call him, asshole, was meeting friends in the area. I told him I would be in Brooklyn too and that we should get a drink. I never expected him to come. As I said, he's stood me up before."

"You said you were invisible to him. He wouldn't have walked into this bar if he didn't see how beautiful you are."

"He looks at me like I'm one of the guys. I want him to look at me like I'm one of the girls."

"Sex and emotions don't always have to go hand in hand. I've hooked up with plenty of women and we both walked away satisfied and didn't need to exchange numbers and talk about it afterwards." Her eyes are set on mine, hanging on every word. "Look, Virginia. If he showed up, he has some interest, but I know his type. It's not to have a conversation and romantic walks with you on the beach."

Absorbing what I'm saying, she ponders a moment, and then asks, "You're saying that just because he talks to me doesn't mean he wants more than sex with me?"

"Exactly."

"I might be okay with this." Her eyes widen, the light at the end of the tunnel coming into full few. "What you said. I need to do sex things without worry and just have fun. Then he'll see me as more than the numbers girl. If I keep it light and then make my move and seduce him, he won't be able to resist."

"That's not really what I was say—"

"This is perfect. Hardy, you're amazing." She sets her sights on me now. "I need your help since you're so good at separating sex from emotion." I should be upset that she sees me this way, but her train of thought intrigues me. "I have a proposition for you."

The only problem I see is that my emotions are so entangled in her that I'm not sure if they're hers or mine anymore. I need separation from her to get proper perspective on what she's really saying. There might be an insult hidden in there, but Katie's advice is not the greatest. She clearly needs my help. I finish my drink and set the glass down. "Go on."

Fidgeting, she says, "I want you to look at something."

"Shoot."

She reaches into her purse and pulls out a photo, then sets it on the table and pushes it toward me. "Look at this."

I pick the photo up and stare at it. It's not a flattering photo—some girl with thick-lensed glasses and braids, an odd orange tint to her hair and headgear. To add more salt to this poor girl's wound, she's wearing a canary yellow turtleneck and purple sweatshirt over it. Glancing up, I put the photo back down. "What is this? Who is this?"

"That's me." She actually manages to hold a straight face when she confesses this.

Grabbing the picture back from the table, I hold it up again. "This is you?" I fail at keeping the astonishment from my voice.

"It is. Senior year in high sch—"

"Senior year? Holy shit." *Oops.* "I mean, wow. You've changed." Looking at her suit, I add, "Mostly."

Shock rolls over her and she grabs her jacket by the lapels and looks down. "What? You don't like my suit?"

"Ummm, it's okay."

When her shoulders sag, I add, "I mean it could be worse."

"Not really by the sound of it. Geez. As if I didn't feel bad enough—"

"I'm sorry. I don't mean to hurt your feelings. I'm just in shock."

"Am I that hideous in the photo?"

"You were never hideous. You were just hiding behind," I start to say, moving my finger over the top of it, "a lot of shit. There's a lot going on here."

"That's why I need your help."

"How can I help you?" I ask not sure where this is going.

"I want your help to win Lowry."

"What's a Lowry?"

"The asshole. That's a Lowry."

Whoa. Whoa. "Whoa. Back up. You want my help winning the attention of that asshole from last night?"

She eagerly nods with a wide smile. "Yes. Exactly."

"Maybe I'm a bit slow, but let me get this straight. You want me to help you somehow get the attention of some guy who doesn't deserve your attention, much less your time of day?"

"Yes."

"Why?"

"Because you know how to get everyone's attention without even trying and then you know all that other stuff."

"What other stuff?"

"The sex stuff."

This time, my eyes go wide before they narrow in utter confusion. "What sex stuff?" Oh man, that pink I love so much colors her cheeks. How does she work the bravado shy girl thing so well? She's not even aware of how she affects men. Unicorn.

Leaning over the table, she glances around to make sure no one hears her. "Last night. What we did last night."

Dot.

Dot.

Connect.

"You want me to teach you sex stuff?" I didn't think my eyes could go wider but now they're practically hanging out in disbelief.

She nods.

I repeat, "You want me to teach you sex stuff to get the attention of that asshole who doesn't deserve your attention, nor time of day?"

She nods again. "Will you help me?" I'm not sure how long I've been staring at her, but it's long enough for her to clap her hands in front of my face. "You still with me?"

"How?"

"How what?" She sits back down, looking a little confused herself.

Shaking my head, I ask, "How do you want me to teach you?"

The way she talks about this as if this is so ordinary, like we're figuring out where to order takeout tonight. "I've been thinking about it. You made me realize last night that it would be like lessons in love, in romance."

"In seduction?"

"Yes."

"You understand that's nuts, right?"

"I do, but what I'm doing now isn't working." Looking down, she holds her jacket out. "At all. I need help. Your help. You get any woman you want. Women throw themselves at you. You know how to read their wants and needs. You know how to make a woman feel special without feeling dirty."

"Unless they want that."

That makes her laugh. "Yes, unless they want to feel dirty."

"Hey, Hardy?" Eddie calls from behind the bar, and waves me over.

We both look over and then back at each other. I say, "They need backup."

"What do you say? Will you help me?"

"I'm not even sure what this entails."

She pushes the photo back toward me. "When is your next night off?"

"Sunday."

"We can talk then, go over the details. You can decide after that. If you say no, I won't blame you. But if you say yes," she says, her excitement growing, "we can plot it all out, set the rules and such."

Standing up when Eddie calls me again, I run my hand through my hair. "This is crazy."

She stands as well, close to me, too far for my liking. "I can tell you like living dangerously."

I don't like when the danger involves my heart, but I know I'm going to accept the challenge, ready to put it on the line. "I don't do things on dares."

"Then what will get you to do this?"

"I like homemade lasagna." I'm a mighty good cook, but I might just have fun with this, and score a home-cooked meal out of this nutball idea.

"Done. How's seven?"

I like her too much to say no. "That works." I hand her my phone. "I'll text you directions to my place."

She quickly adds her number into my contacts and says, "I put my number under my new favorite drink." Handing it back to me, she bounces once on her feet and then lifts to hug me.

My arms wrap around her and I inhale the sensual vanilla I've come to love into my lungs. My body relaxes, and I wish we weren't in the middle of the bar. Stepping back abruptly, I say, "I've gotta go."

"Thank you."

I nod and head to the bar. When I look back at her, she's heading for the door.

Eddie says, "Jagger called in sick."

"Is he?"

He laughs. "I think he's dick deep in the girl from the corner deli."

TMI. I look at the door, hoping to see Virginia once more, but she's gone. "I'll fill in. Just cover a few more minutes." I dash to the door and push it open. When my feet land on the snow covered sidewalk, I look right and then left, searching for her. When my eyes land on her great body, I call out, "Hey Virginia?"

Snow is falling, little white dots covering her hair when she turns with a flourish, a sweet smile on her lips. My heart hurts just looking at her. She's so beautiful. I open my mouth to tell her—*You were never invisible to me*—but that doesn't come out. Instead, I chicken out, and say, "See you Sunday."

Her smiles grows and she replies, "See you Sunday, Hardy."

Chapter Seven

My night is more than cocktails. Along with drinks, it's quite busy with offers. When I serve twelve tequila shots to a bachelorette party, the favor is returned in the form of an insulting two-hundred-dollar offer to strip. I'm worth way more than two hundred bucks. And if I were to strip, it wouldn't be for money, but for fun and hopefully sex at the end. What the fuck am I talking about? Oh, and no offense to any strippers who might be reading this. Virginia has my mind all mucked up tonight. She wants me to give her lessons in love. I'm seriously the luckiest fucker to walk this planet.

Back to the offers . . . when I serve a merlot, an offer of a blow job comes back instead of a tip. A bottle of tequila celebrating a girls' night out is delivered and with hands that lean more on the pawing side they offer to take me home and ravage my body like, and I quote, "a dingo to a baby." I tried to shake the disturbing thought from my brain, but when I couldn't, I didn't bother to answer. I just walked away.

I'm too tired to fend them off, so it's time for me to go

before I regret staying and doing something I'll regret even more in the morning. The guys can handle the last hour before closing. The temps have dropped even lower than earlier and I didn't bring my heavy jacket. The two blocks I cover in the snow at a breakneck pace keeps the chill at bay.

The streets are quiet, which I like, and if I listen carefully, I can almost hear the snow falling. I stop in front of my building and look up, closing my eyes, and listen. *Hardy, I want you.* Her words from last night echo through the night and down my street in the wind. Opening my eyes, snowflakes land on my lashes. Lessons in seduction. "Woohoo!" I jump up, feeling like I just won the lottery. Seduction. I'm the king of it. I cannot wait for Sunday night. I punch in the building code. A little wining. A little dining. A little romance and a lot of seduction. Now that is what I call a jackpot.

When I unlock my apartment, the place is dark, the only light coming from the streetlight at the corner of the block, which is too far to be a bother. I toss my keys in the bowl and shut the door. Standing in the middle of my living room, something new washes through me. A feeling I've never felt living here. I brush it away and go about winding down. It's hard to do when you were wired thirty minutes prior.

I take a shower, hoping the warm water relaxes my muscles and my mind. It does neither. Neither does Virginia. Speaking of muscles, Big Richard is hard. *Again.* Wrapping my hand firmly around my cock, I start slow with images of that pink, my newest favorite color. My speed picks up when we kiss—soft, plush, willing lips. *So close. So fucking close.* Her lower lips even softer, wetter. My fingers slide through and fuck her all over again . . . and I'm coming. Fuck me. Fuck.

My free hand is against the tile, my head under the shower spray, and I loosen my grip. God damn it. She's going to be the death of me, and Big Richard. We'll see who can survive the longest come Sunday night.

***

Wednesday. Check.

Thursday. Friday. Check. Check.

Saturday. *Fuck.*

I'm in no mood to be here. I pull at the noose around my neck and order another whiskey. Neat. Stepping off to the side, but sticking close to the bar, my comfort zone, I survey the room. That's when I'm blindsided or maybe it's more of a sideline tackle. Either way, I didn't see it coming. *Or her,* more specifically.

"Hardy Richard. It's been too long."

Not long enough. "Has it, Isabella?"

"You were always so funny." It's impressive how she manages to say that without smiling. Maybe the Botox has gone two layers deep, which is about as deep as Isabella Collins, formerly Isabella Treaton when I dated her, gets.

"My parents call it sarcasm. You might remember it got me in a lot of trouble."

"You were always in a lot of trouble." She touches my tie to straighten it, but I cover her hand and kindly remove it. "But what's the fun in playing it safe? I like this burgundy tie. It's so festive for the season."

I ignore the compliment. They always come with ulterior motives that I'm not interested in getting involved in again. "As for playing it safe, you have a kid, and a husband who commutes from Connecticut. Do you also have a dog and a Mercedes?"

"A Cavalier King Charles, more specifically, and a Mercedes GLS SUV in Iridium Silver."

"You don't exactly walk on the wild side."

"You think because you're single, I'm still assuming by that bare ring finger, and you live in Brooklyn that you're living the high life?"

"I didn't say I was, but I'm living, experiencing, and I'm better off than I was four years ago."

"Better off?" She appears reflective as she sips her champagne. When her light blue eyes hit mine, she asks, "We had some good times together, right?"

"We were alike in many ways, but we were terrible together." God's honest truth. We were lucky the cops were never called during one of our blowout fights. The woman knows how to use words that cut right to your core. She also has always had a philandering problem. That's why it's just better to avoid that catastrophe of locking oneself down to another altogether. Then when you fuck around with someone, no one else gets hurt.

"I remember us so differently. Living in the city with great paying jobs right out of college. You had that great apartment with the view. So many good memories were made there."

"Our family's connections afforded us our degrees and careers. It was never what I wanted. I was working to protect the Richard name while destroying myself."

"You didn't seem unhappy."

I finish my whiskey in one go. "I was drowning in my life, waking up every day wishing I was living another."

Eyeing my empty glass, judgment creases her forehead as she raises an eyebrow. A motion I'm surprised she can still make. "You're doing a good job now."

"I have different reasons to drown out tonight."

"You sound bitter, Hardy. It's sad to see someone with

so much potential throw it all away on a walk up in Brooklyn and a run down bar."

I set my glass on the tray behind the bar and walk away. It's a bad habit I've developed. Once I turned twenty-eight, I ran out of patience for people who carry negativity around like the latest designer bag. Isabella Collins is the queen of holding my past against me. She was always one for the low blow.

"Hardy?"

I stop walking, the exit is so close, but slips from my reach when I hear my mother's voice. Plastering a big smile on my face, I turn around. "Mother. I was just looking for you." Lies to appease.

Her face lights up. She's actually a really good mom. Isabella just has a way of souring a good mood. I greet my mom with a kiss to her cheek and a hug. She embraces me and then leans back to get a good look at me. "Honey, you look so handsome in dark gray. Your suit fits you perfectly. Is this custom made? Though you're too skinny living in the city. It's so competitive there. You should move back to Connecticut and let me feed you home cooked meals every night."

The suit is Gucci and tailored to me, but I know she's more worried about my eating habits. Chuckling, I say, "I feel better when I'm fit."

Wrapping her arm around my back, she leans her head on my shoulder. "I'm allowed to worry about my youngest. You don't need anything else from me, so give me that. Okay?"

"Yes, Mother."

This time she laughs. Loud enough that a few people look our way. She has always had a free spirit, not caring what others thought of her. What she doesn't realize is that everyone adores her.

Virginia's laugh rings through my ears and an image of her pops into my head. My mother whispers, "Are you seeing anyone?"

The woman has a second sense for when her kids meet someone worth seeing twice. "Nah."

Her hands are clasped together in front of her mouth, a smile rivaling the Grand Canyon, and I actually see a mischievous delight dancing in her eyes. That or I've been reading too many Playboy stories online. That's probably it. Yeah, yeah, I read it for the articles. I get enough of the *real* thing in *real* life. I don't need pictures of women who've been photoshopped to get me off. I've got enough offers and spank bank material in my head to do the job just fine.

Damn, I forgot I'm with my mom. I shudder, ridding the images now circulating around my brain, I say, "I haven't seen Dad yet."

"He's here somewhere," she replies, looking around the ballroom. "We've raised over five hundred thousand already."

"Big donations."

"Yes, the fundraiser is doing well. Can I bother you for a donation?"

"No bother. How much do you want?"

"Five thousand would be great. Ten would be better."

I reach for my checkbook, pulling it from the inside pocket of my jacket. "Pen?" She hands one to me. I write out a check for the full amount hinted at and hand it to her.

"Thank you, Son. Now, go get something to eat before I have to force feed you some of my pot roast."

"You don't have to force-feed me your pot roast. I'd take it happily."

"Maybe you can come for dinner on Sunday night?"

Sunday. *Virginia.* "I can't Sunday, but maybe another one?"

A pat on the back is followed by a laugh. She says, "Yes, you're welcome any Sunday, Son. Now go eat. The food is being served."

I find my place card right next to Isabella, and I have a sneaking suspicion it wasn't there originally. I'm tempted to cut out early now that I've made my donation, but I haven't seen my dad yet and the lecture I would get for not staying isn't worth it. I spy my parents sitting down five tables to the left front, closer to the stage.

"I thought you'd be gone by now, Hardy."

Pulling my chair out just as a plate is set in front of me, I reply, "Thank you," to the waiter, and to Isabella, "Soon."

"You act like this is painful for you. Are you that much of a snob these days?"

I almost spit out the water I just drank. "Me? Wow, I'm not sure what to say to that." Looking at the seat next to her, I ask, "Alone?"

"Unintended."

"Matt always loved his work."

She takes her glass and finishes the rest of her champagne. "Yes, he does."

I sense her shift in mood, but she has a way of twisting things to turn them back on me and I'm not in the mood to justify my life to her anymore. "If you'll excuse me," I say, pushing back from the table. "I'm going to say hello to my dad."

"Good seeing you, Hardy."

When I look back at her, her eyes seem fixed on her plate, her fork in hand still on the table. "See you around, Isabella."

I walk up behind my dad, and pat him on the shoulder. "Hey, Dad."

He's always been strict, not like my mom. They were definitely an opposites attract couple. Tonight he's smiling and has a beer buzz by the looks of it. "Hardy, my boy." He stands, setting his napkin down, and hugs me. "Good to see you, Son."

"Good to see you, too. You look good."

Wiggling back and forth, he tugs at his belt. "Well, the old man's still got it."

I hear my mom laugh. "Don't encourage him, Hardy. He's already a handful since he retired."

"What? When did you retire?" I ask, shocked to hear my workaholic father has left his top priority in life.

"Last week. I didn't make a big fuss to you kids. You have enough going on."

"I always want to know what's going on with you and this is big news. Congratulations."

"Thanks, Son," he replies jollily. "Maybe I'll come visit you at The Hideaway. We can have a drink."

My dad's never been there before. My mom has come by a few times before opening hours. She approved but left before as she says, "The ladies show up to bed me." Besides being grossed out that my mom even said, "bed me," I quickly escorted her out to catch a cab because she's right and no mom should have to witness their son in all his charming glory make the ladies swoon. "Sure, Dad. Just let me know. Drinks are on me."

"Sure thing."

"I'm going to take off." I shake his hand and hug my mom over her shoulder. "Good to see you."

My dad, unlike his normal uptight self, says, "Don't be a stranger."

"I won't."

"Thank you for the donation," my mom adds. "Love you."

"Love you." I snake through the tables and head out before I get stopped again. There are too many ghosts from my past at this charity event and I much prefer the dark brunette with green eyes haunting my thoughts.

Chapter Eight

5:35 p.m.
    5:36 p.m.
    5:37 p.m.
This is ridiculous.

Why am I a mess over a woman? Since when did I start losing my cool over a chick bringing me food?

There's a knock on the door. I run to answer, then catch myself as soon as I grab hold of the doorknob. Fuck, calm down. I take a deep breath. Play it cool. Play it cool. I look down. My heart may be steadier, but someone else just woke up. Fuck.

I do ten quick jumping jacks and use a trick that's never failed me.

Washington.

Adams.

Jefferson.

Madison.

Monroe.

Adams.

Jackson.

Shit. I've forgotten who comes next. I open the door, and ask, "Which president comes after Jackson?"

She waltzes past me like she's been here a million times. "Van Buren and then Harrison." Setting the glass dish on the kitchen counter, she looks up at me, and smiles. "This is fun. Let's play more."

"Tyler."

"Polk."

"Taylor."

And in unison, we say, "Fillmore."

She laughs, slipping her coat and scarf off. "So dirty."

I hang her stuff up on the hook by the door. "I never thought about it, but now that you say it, Fillmore is dirty." I join her on the other side of the bar, keeping the marble counter between us. Also, just in case Big Richard is still awake, he'll need cover.

"Why are we reciting the Presidents?"

Shrugging, I play it off. "Just keeping my mind sharp."

She opens a bag she set down with the lasagna, which smells amazing by the way. Pulling out a bottle of wine, she says, "I love brain games. My favorite is Memory."

I sit on the barstool and watch her as she unpacks. Her expression is happy and carefree as she talks about the game. I like hearing about her favorite things. It tells me more about her, and feels personal, instead of the bullshit a lot of people talk about. She asks, "Have you played?"

"I played as a kid."

"This is much more challenging than the card game when you were little." She twists the cap off the wine, and adds, "Wine?"

"Yes." I watch her work around my kitchen, making herself at home.

She pulls two glasses from where they hang upside

down inside a cabinet before returning to the wine and pouring. She sets a glass in front of me and waits. "I hope you like it. I asked a wine guy to help me at the liquor store. He said it would be a good pairing with lasagna."

"A sommelier?"

"No, just the guy who owns the corner shop down by my work."

Swirling it around from the base of the glass, I can't stop from smiling. "You didn't have to do all this, but please know, I think it's very thoughtful."

"I'm asking a lot of you. The least I can do is get you drunk first." She laughs at her own joke.

It was funny, but that she enjoyed it so much is funnier, so I laugh in response. "So you're trying to butter me up or get me drunk?"

"Maybe both."

"What exactly do you have in mind?"

"I think I'll feed you, and keep your glass full. Let you relax while I clean up after. And then hopefully we get started."

"I meant the lessons, not how you plan to take advantage of me." I take my first sip of the wine after letting it breathe, although not quite as long as I should. "I'm not as easy as you seem to think."

"Really? We were in your office not two hours after meeting."

"I found you adorably fascinating."

She can only hold our locked eyes a few seconds more before her gaze lowers to the dish on the counter. "Are you hungry?"

"Famished."

She looks up and her tongue dips out to wet her lower lip before it tugs under her teeth. She doesn't realize how sexy she really is—a bombshell that hits you when you're weak. The air is noticeably thicker. She exhales a heavier breath, but this time her eyes stay on mine. "Lasagna?"

Slowly, I come around the counter and stand next to her. She leans her hip against the counter, facing me, and I say, "Lesson one. The art of flirting."

"I told you the other night that I'm not a total virgin. I've had dates. I've kissed plenty of men. I've made out with them."

"This isn't about sex or making out. This is an art form. If you want my help, and I really hope you do, then we start from the beginning."

Tucking some hair behind her ear, I let my gaze drift to her lips and then lower, running over every inch of her without touching her at all. Her sweater is thin as well as her bra, her nipples hardening before me. The deep V displays her delicate neck and teases me with a peek at her collarbone. I'm tempted to run my tongue along the curve of her neck and lower. It's hard to hold back after tasting heaven.

When she raises her arm across her body and holds onto the opposite shoulder, I whisper, "No. No hiding from me."

"But—"

"No. Vulnerability is sexy. It's genuine and real. You're presenting yourself to me, showing me what's in here." I rub her temple gently before taking her hand and kissing the palm.

"What do you see?"

"I see the shy girl who hides behind bulky suits and numbers. I also see the woman who wants those layers peeled away and her body bare."

She's breathless, her chest rising and falling quickly. "I thought we were going to flirt."

"Flirting is foreplay. Are you turned on?"

Her gaze lowers this time, and my body awakens in reaction. I don't hide my erection this time. I want her to see what she does to me. I want her to know how much she turns me on. Reaching for my wine glass, I take it while picking up hers. I hand it to her and make a toast, "To good wine and even better company." Our glasses clink together and our gazes hold while we drink. "Let me serve you dinner."

"But I thought I would."

"You made it and brought it over here. Let me do something for you."

"You are, Hardy. You're helping me so much. Lowry will not be able to turn me down. I just know it."

The magic disappears from the mere mention of that asshole. He's a glaring reminder that feelings aren't always returned. Sometimes they remain one-sided. "Let me do it anyway. Table or couch?"

She looks around the room, and says, "You have a great apartment. Couch."

"Thanks." I struggle to keep the defeat out of my tone. "You go sit. Relax. I'll finish in here."

Moving into the living room, she walks around the space slowly, looking at everything from the knickknacks on the bookcases to staring out the window at the street below. "You're only two floors up and there is absolutely no outside noise. You must have some nice windows."

"Are we really talking about windows right now?" I've heated the lasagna and deliver the plate as she sits on the couch.

"I guess I'm a little awkward. Sorry. I get caught up in the unimportant stuff when I'm nervous."

With my plate in hand, I sit next to her on the couch.

"See? That right there is exactly what I don't want. I don't want your apologies or for you to be nervous. I just want your—" *Body.* "—friendship."

"You have it." She leans back with her glass in hand. "Can I ask you something personal?"

"You can ask me anything. As for answering, that remains to be seen."

"Were you always this confident? This comfortable with who you are?"

"No," I say, chuckling from the unexpected questions. "I went through an awkward stage in tenth grade. My head finally fit my body, my teeth were straight, and I grew over four inches—my body, dirty girl—and kind of grew into me, into this body."

Rubbing her palms down her thighs, she picks her glass back up and drinks. When she sets it back down, she says, "I like the body I grew into. Is that rude of me to admit?"

She's so damn sexy. "No, not at all. I want to see you more comfortable in that body though."

"Me too." She takes a bite of her lasagna.

"What is your favorite part of your body, the one thing or things you enjoy showing off?"

"My boobs."

"You have fantastic tits."

"Hardy," she cautions while laughing.

"I only speak the truth."

As much as she doesn't want to admit that the compliment pleases her because of the vulgar language, she loves it just as much. With another bite perched on her fork, she asks, "What's your favorite part of your body?"

"I know you think I'm going to say my dick, but I'm not."

She giggles. "What is it then?"

"You tell me."

"Cheater."

"I'm the teacher. I make the rules."

Looking me over, she says, "Your fingers. I like how strong and deft they are."

I wiggle them just to add to the memory of how they wiggled inside her earlier this week. Heaven.

"Your eyes because of the hazel color and the way they change, but mostly because of the way they look at me."

"How do they look at you?"

"Like I'm beautiful."

"You are so beautiful that parts of my soul ache to touch parts of yours."

She takes in a shaky breath and swallows hard. "You can't go around saying things like that even though you're teaching me how. Because for a brief second, I believed you."

"You can believe me for more than a second. I was telling you the truth. Nothing is sexier than the truth shared between two trusting," I say, moving closer to her on the couch, "consensual adults." My breathing changes, the mere proximity to her affecting me. "I want to kiss you."

"I thought we were practicing flirting?"

"Practicing?" I sit forward, resting my forearms on my knees. "Yes, right. Practicing."

"We can move on from that if you want. If you think I'm ready."

Ready. I'm so ready, but there's no way I'm rushing my time with her away. "We'll take it slow, and get it right."

"How am I doing so far?"

"Grand. You almost fooled me, but I saw through the act." I'm such an idiot.

"How old are you, Hardy Richard?"

"Twenty-eight. How old are you?"

"Twenty-five in three weeks."

"You were born around Christmas?"

"People call me a Christmas baby, but. I was born on Christmas Eve. My mom said I wasn't due until New Year's Day, but I couldn't wait to start my life."

"Your mom sounds a lot like mine."

"I bet you were a hellion." She rests her head back on the couch, going and looking all beautiful again.

A smirk slides into place. "Why do you say that?"

"You're handsome and personable. You're running a successful business so clearly you're smart. You tick all the boxes of having the world fall at your feet."

Leaning back next to her, I kick my feet up on the coffee table. "Everyone has their struggles. Mine just came a little after yours."

The mood shifts and she asks, "When did you lose your virginity?"

"Sixteen."

"That's not as early as I was thinking. You're such a pro at this relationship stuff that I thought you'd say something like fourteen or younger. How'd you lose it? Was it romantic with a girl you loved?"

"Nope. It was at Clara Duncan's sweet sixteen party. The party was going on upstairs and we snuck down to the basement and ended up having sex on a ratty old couch down there. And since I know you're going to ask—no, it wasn't good and I sucked. I came as soon as I touched the tip of my dick to her. I fumbled and thrust into her fast when I panicked. She almost screamed. I never thought to prepare her or to ease in. Yeah, it was pretty awful."

She's laughing so hard that it takes a minute for her to

get enough air gathered to ask, "Did you date her a long time?"

"I dated her until she broke up with me the next day for Chad Mackenzie. Once it got around school that she put out for me, every dickwad in school was after her."

"That's too bad."

"Not really." I laugh. The story is too ridiculous not to. Now. Hindsight and all that. "The hottest senior in school approached me a week later asking me to . . ." I stop and look at Virginia.

"What?"

I chuckle. "To help her out."

Tilting her head, she rolls her eyes, and teases, "I thought I was different."

You are. "You are." Shit. I watch her for a reaction, praying it's a good one.

Her fingers fumble together in her lap, that sweetest of pinks seen even in the low light reaching us from the kitchen. "You say the nicest things, Hardy. You're really good at this flirting thing."

Sighing, I realize she thinks I'm saying this as part of the plan, that it's put on and not real. I take my wine and drink. "Thanks," I reply, disappointment coating my words. "We should eat before it gets cold." I never was good at hiding my emotions. Maybe it's because I hate lying, and liars even more. I try to live my life as honestly as possible. When I screw up, I own it. When I succeed, I own that shit too.

This game we're playing is dangerous, but it seems only to my heart. So as much as I want to tell her I'm starting to have feelings for her, I'm not ready to lose her. She's clearly into the asshole, so not only do I find myself now lying, but I've also become the liar I loathe.

Stealing a glimpse of her, I realize—She's totally worth it.

Chapter Nine

Silence stretched across dinner, and I hated it. I don't want this for us. After another few bites, I tell her, "This might be the best lasagna I've ever had." Truth.

That brightens her spirit. "Really?"

"Really."

"It's my great-grandmother's recipe. She wasn't Italian but she once told me about a torrid love affair she had with a chef while visiting Rome in the twenties."

Things begin to turn around for us both. I do love me some sexual banter. "Torrid, huh?"

"I think that means she had sex with him against her family's wishes."

"I think that means a lot more. How do you feel about torrid?"

"With you?" She sets her plate down and takes a sip of her wine before sitting back and tucking her legs under her.

She looks good on my couch, making me wonder what she'll look like on my bed. "We can do torrid?"

"I think I have a few other lessons to learn first."

"I think you're doing just fine."

"That's because you're being nice."

I set my plate down. "Stop saying that, okay?" Tapping her leg, I make sure she's looking in my eyes to see I mean what I say. "When I say something to you, I mean it. I'm not saying it to make you feel better or on false pretenses. If you feel better because of it, great. That's a bonus, but I don't lie and I'm not lying to you."

"I'm sorr—"

"I don't need you to apologize either. I want you to relax and enjoy our time together, like I am."

"It's just so easy with you. It's never been like this before with any of the guys I dated."

"That's because they wanted to fuck you."

The lilt in her voice is heard, the anticipation seen in her eyes. "And what do you want to do?"

Resting my hand on her thigh, she's right. It's easy being with her. "I want to fuck you."

I'm pushed in the chest and fall back on the couch laughing. She's laughing and says, "You're terrible."

"I'm also a guy." When I sit up, I add, "And I want you to find love."

"You mean teach me to find love," she corrects, missing my subtlety altogether.

On the tail end of an exhale, I give her what she wants to hear. "Yes, Virginia. I want to teach you to find love."

"So how am I doing with the flirting?"

"Better than you realize."

She appears pleased. Standing up, she collects our plates. "Would you like more?"

"Definitely," I reply, not talking about the food at all. Watching her in my kitchen, I ask, "What do you want, Virginia?"

She giggles and comes back to the couch. Handing me a second helping of dinner, she adds, "I really want to look back on my life and know I had at least one great love affair that I can reflect on fondly and tell my granddaughters all about."

I'll be your torrid. Just open your eyes, pretty girl.

Her expression turns serious. "Do you think Lowry will be that guy?"

"I think Lowry is the opposite of anything torrid, but it's about what you want. Not what I want."

"I want Lowry."

A heavy realization weighs me down. This woman is going to be the death of me. "Then I'll help you."

"How's Tuesday for lesson two?"

"I can leave work early."

"Or I can come to your work? We can practice the flirting and whatever lesson two is at The Hideaway."

Her dedication is impressive, and I'm not an idiot. "Okay. Just come whenever. I'll take my break after you arrive. We'll get some real life practice in."

Just after nine, she stands. "I should get going. I have a breakfast meeting at seven and it will take me an hour to get home."

Stay. My psychological willing powers don't work as she grabs her coat and slips it on. I take her scarf from the hook. "You have a few servings left. Just reheat and eat though sometimes I like it cold."

"Thanks again . . ." Stay. *Damn.* Still doesn't work. She opens the door and I follow her out. "So I'll see you Tuesday at the bar."

"I look forward to it."

We make our way down the stairs, and I hold the door open for her. We walk out into the night, the cold hitting harder than usual. "I'll get you a cab."

"Thanks."

Walking to the curb, I put my arm out. My street is quiet but just busy enough to have taxis troll looking for fares. One pulls up and Virginia comes to get in. "Hardy?"

Turning to stand close enough for me to inhale her little white breaths puffing between us. "Yeah?"

"My scarf," she says, pointing at my hands.

Oh. "Oh, sorry." I take it in both hands and instead of handing it to her, I bring it around the back of her neck. Pink lips, green eyes with innocence shading the pupils, hair that shines even at night. So utterly tempting to pull her close and kiss her until she sees that I'm doing more than flirting with her.

Her hands cover mine. Those delicate lips part and we stare into each other's eyes. After a few long beats, she whispers, "I had a good time."

"Me too." I cup her face and lean down, closing my eyes. My heart is racing and her breath becomes mine, but I don't kiss her like I want. I angle to the side and kiss her cheek. "Be safe."

I'm not sure if I hear her gulp or it's mine that's filling our ears, but that phrase *the struggle is real* was never so prevalent as it is now. I take a step back and hold the door open for her. Her eyes leave mine and she slips inside the cab. I hand the driver money and tell him to take her home. "Thank you," she says.

I shut the door, tap the top, and move away. Shoving my hands in my pockets, I nod. With a little wave to me, the cab drives away. I watch until the taillights disappear. When I go upstairs, vanilla still lingers, making me smile. I'm going to have to do some soul searching. Who knew one little green-eyed analyst could flip your world upside down without you even realizing it until it's too late?

This situation has turned into a quandary, and as such, I'm going to need to consult with the expert on love —Romeo.

***

Romeo Rossi. The ladies call him The Italian Stallion of The Hideaway. I'm calling on him for advice.

"How can I help you, my friend?" he asks when I take a seat at the bar in front of him. We're open, but at four in the afternoon on a Monday, it's not busy. Yet.

"I need to ask you about something," I start off awkwardly. This is so far out of my comfort zone. Not just the spider web of feelings complicating my life, but asking anyone for advice. I've given plenty of it, but I'm not used to needing it. "There's this girl."

He leans against the wood bar and smiles. "I never thought I'd see the day when the boss himself would need advice from one of us lowly tenders."

"This was a shit idea. Get the whiskey. I can tell I'm going to need it."

While he pours me a glass, I say, "I wouldn't come to just anyone. I'm coming to you because you've had long-term relationships and one broken engagement. I don't think the other guys know the names of half the women they sleep with, so you're the chosen one."

"I'm honored." He pushes the glass toward me.

After shooting the amber liquid, I set the glass down, and say, "I met her here."

"Whoa!" His body jerks as if he's been hit in the chest. "You live by two rul—"

"I know. That's why I can't wrap my head around

what's going on. I have," I start to say, but pause, not believing that I'm about to say it out loud for the first time.

"You have what?"

"Feelings."

"Holy shit, Hardy. How'd that happen? Is she hot?"

"So hot. Wet dreams hot. And I really have no fucking clue how this happened." I rub my temples. "One minute I was kissing her leading into more, and then the next she's telling me she's a virgin and I'm offering to dance with her instead."

"Instead of what?" he asks shocked.

"Sex."

"What the fuck? You passed up sex with her because she was a virgin?" Now he's rubbing his temples as if he can't comprehend this actually happening.

"I wasn't going to fuck her for the first time on a desk. She deserves better than that."

"I get that, but wow. I'm seriously impressed with your restraint." Resting his hands wide on the bar, he asks, "Maybe you have feelings for her because she's a virgin."

"No, I almost find that aspect more intimidating. I mean really. When was the last time you were with a virgin?"

"Last week."

He answers so casually that I make sure I heard right. "You were?"

"Sure. So I get what you're saying. You can't just bend them over and have them begging for more when they're virgins."

"Exactly. Virginia deserves romance. She deserves to be wooed into bed and then made love to."

"Let me get this straight. She's a hot virgin named Virginia?"

"The irony wasn't lost on me either. Anyway, I haven't

been with a virgin in a long time. Those aren't the typical women I hook up with.""You're overthinking it. All they want is to be made love to. Once you get that first time out of the way, it's like they're making up for lost time. I'm fucking exhausted. We've been going at it three times, sometimes up to five times a day since I popped that cherry."

I stand up and take a step back. "We might have crossed that line of what I need and what I don't need to know."

Romeo laughs. "We got off track, but if you have feelings for her, even developing ones that you aren't ready to admit to, you owe it to yourself to see if something's there. I know you live by your two rules and they've served you well, but maybe it's time to see if there's something more with this girl."

"Stop making so much sense. You're supposed to be the one telling me to back as far away as I can."

Shrugging, he says, "You don't ever come to me for advice. These roles are usually reversed, so when you say you have feelings for a chick, I know it's serious." Swiping the glass he turns and sets it in the sink behind him. "Even the greatest of men eventually fall."

"Sounds like I'm heading into battle?"

He chuckles. "The battle's already lost, my friend. It's time to raise that surrender flag and give love a chance."

I roll my eyes. "You always were a sap."

"A sap in love. Takes one to know one."

"I'm not in love," I mumble while walking to the office.

Behind me, he calls out, "Keep telling yourself that."

I will. *Oh, I will.*

Chapter Ten

The seed has been planted, and now it's growing. As if from sheer will and want, it's branching out beyond a thought. It has bloomed into action.

I slide my hand out from under the Tequila Sunrise sitting in front of me.

No one has to know.

No strings attached.

Sex for no other reason than to feel good.

We'd walk away with our loads lightened. Literally and figuratively.

"I appreciate the offer, but I'm working." I'm not lying, I do appreciate the offer, but I am working. And saving my break time for Virginia.

"You sure. I could really use the company."

Under any other circumstances, I'd take her into the back without hesitation. Curves to kill. Blond hair pulled back into a ponytail begging to be pulled harder. Lips that had to be injected they were so full—ready to lick. Ready to suck. Fuck. She's a flight attendant on a layover, for Christ's sake. "I'm sure, but I'll buy your drink." It was the least I could do.

"Thank you, but I would have preferred a good time. Maybe next time I'm in town."

"Stop by."

I watch as she walks to the door and disappears into the night—lonely and horny. "Fuck."

Eddie asks, "What's up?"

"Did you see the blonde?"

"Couldn't miss her. Gorgeous."

"I just turned her down."

"Are you sick? Not feeling well?"

"I'm starting to wonder that myself."

He says, "More importantly, why didn't you introduce me?"

"Because she wanted a man, not a boy."

"Speaking of, how's the de-virgining going? Or would it be un-virgining?"

"Romeo has a big fucking mouth."

Eddie is laughing too hard to notice I'm not. He finally says, "I think he was in too much shock to keep it to himself. None of us has ever seen you have genuine feelings for a woman. He needed to talk to someone."

Another eye roll hits. "Who'd you tell?"

"Me?" he asks all innocently. "Only Clive."

Closing my eyes, I shake my head. "Fuck, now everyone will know."

"He said he'd keep it on the down low. About down lows, does she?"

I send him a harsh glare. When I don't respond, he keeps chattering, and I wonder if he'd keep going even if I wasn't here. Eddie's the most personable bartender here. The ladies love him because he charms them with stories, keeping them entertained and laughing. He rakes in the tips and I rake in the money. Laughter is like an aphrodisiac. The guy scores almost as much as Romeo.

"The floor behind the bar needs mopping. Keep rattling on like that and you'll have yourself a new job."

He's still laughing as he starts cutting limes. I head to the office to pass time until Virginia shows up, annoyed with these guys.

***

Not sure how long I'm in the back balancing the books, but when I hear a knock, I look up surprised by the sound. "Come in."

I'm greeted with green eyes and long hair, jeans and sneakers under a navy blue puffy coat that hides her figure. I decide to greet her a little differently, taking full advantage of our arrangement. Meeting her just inside the door, I shut it and lean over. Lifting her chin, I kiss her without reservation, just the way I've wanted to kiss her since that first night.

When I pull back, her eyes are closed, her hands on my chest, and she leans her forehead against me. "What was that for?""Lesson two." I lie, something I'm becoming too good at when I'm around her.

Leaning against the door, she smiles. "I think I'm going to like lesson two."

"I've got thirty minutes."

Her arms go around my neck. "Let's not waste a second." She lifts up and presses her lips to mine.

Angling my head, I capture her lips more fully with mine, parting them just enough to get a taste of her forbidden heaven. After she told me she had a crush on that asshole, I didn't think I'd get this chance again. It's crazy that I do, so like she said, I'm not going to waste a second.

Weaving my hands into her hair, I hold her to me as our mouths part, need and instinct trumping slow and steady.

My body presses against hers and she moves against mine. Hands find my middle and tighten. A soft, kitten like moan is swallowed when it transfers from her to me. I tilt her head to the side and my mouth trails over her cheek, jaw, and then lower to her neck. But the hood of her coat blocks the access I need. Pulling away, my breath comes hard, hers matching mine as we stare into each other's eyes. I say, "I want your coat off."

Snaps fly open before I finish my demand. I take the zipper pull under her chin and drag it slowly down over her chest, letting my knuckles graze her chest. Her T-shirt is soft and no barrier is felt. Shit. I look down quickly, holding her coat open at the top. "Are you wearing a bra?"

Her tongue slips out, wetting her lips. Holy fuck. Kissing. Lesson two is kissing. Only kissing. "Nope."

That damn pop of the *P* drives me wild. I cup her face and am about to devour her delicious lips, but stop just when ours meet. "You're a damn temptress, but so damn innocent at the same time. How are you so perfect?" Unicorn.

Giggling, her body shakes, her eyes are alight, all the stars in the night sky caught inside. "I think I could argue that perfect part." When I have a hold of my hormones, I release her and stand back, giving her room to breathe. Her mouth twists and then she says, "I think a few past boyfriends could argue that as well."

With her coat open, she lets it slide down her arms. I hang it on the coat rack and watch as she sits on the loveseat. I'd follow her but I need Big Richard to calm down a bit.

Kissing. *Only kissing.*

Moving to my desk, I sit in the chair in front of it, keeping a safe distance from her tempting nips. I mean lips. "This is gonna be harder than I thought."

"I think it already is," she replies, glancing to my lap.

"Just ignore him."

"Him?" She sits up excitedly, leaning closer. "Tell me about him. Does he have a name?"

Fuck. "Stop staring. He loves the attention. He'll never calm down if you keep looking at him with your lips parted like that."

When her gaze lifts to mine, she smirks. *Smirks.* Stolen right from my playbook kind of smirk. She has some nerve throwing it back at me. She's a quick learner. I need to remember that. Sexpot.

Dragging her finger over her bottom lip, it pouts out just a little before she asks, "Like this? Does he like lips parted like this?" Sucking the tip of her finger into her mouth, she pulls it out. "Or like that? Which does he prefer?"

I stand abruptly and walk to the door. Opening the door, I say, "I'll be right back." The door is shut behind me, my back against it as I settle my racing heart and hard-on. I need a drink. "Enchantress with her tempting kisses and eager eyes," I mumble as I walk. Whiskey. My target is in sight. I grab a glass, flip it on the bar and it lands bottom side down. I reach for the Jack Daniels and flip the bottle in the air, catching it by the neck and turning it down to fill my glass.

"Everything okay, boss?" Eddie asks.

"Nope." I mimic Virginia's answer from a few minutes earlier. I don't pop the *P* because that would be girly. I do down the whiskey before refilling it though. "Can you bring a Paloma to the office?"

"No problem." I walk off, but he calls out, "Hey." I turn back. "She's hot. You might want to take the bottle."

"You're right." I grab hold of it.

"Want me to inventory that bottle?"

"Sure do."

"On it."

Cutting across the room, I push open the back door and wait for it. I take a deep breath and exhale before opening the office door. Virginia stands, her fingertips tucked into her pockets. "Everything okay?" she asks nervously. My insides ache just looking at her. So damn beautiful. "Does my kissing suck?"

"Fuck." I down the shot.

"Hardy?"

I rush forward, setting the bottle down along the way. Taking hold of her, I kiss her hard, wanting her to realize her kisses are the opposite of sucking, and as someone who is a good judge of a woman's sucking, I'd know. Then she does that little moan again and my hands slide up her ribs and I cup her breasts. Her head falls back, and exhales, "Yes. God, yes."

"Hardy. Say it."

"Hardy. Yes, Hardy. It feels so good with your hands on me."

Rubbing my thumb over her nipples, the cotton between us too thin to hide the pebbling. Her neck is delicate and waiting for my mouth, which I'm more than happy to tend to. Starting at the curve of her shoulder, I lick her sweet, vanilla skin to her ear. Just as I take her earlobe between my teeth, a knock on the office door intrudes.

My body tenses just as I was starting to relax. "I'm sorry."

"Don't worry. I'll be right here waiting for you."

I want to kick whoever's ass it is for making me leave her like this. My dick is throbbing and answering the damn door isn't going to help my situation. I swing it open. "What?"

Eddie's standing there holding a drink. "Your Paloma."

Oh. "Shit," I start apologetically. "Sorry. Thanks."

"It's okay." His eyes drift over my shoulder and an eyebrow lifts. "Let us know if you need anything else."

"I'm good. We're good." I'm talking way too fast. His attention turns to me, his forehead crinkled like he's inter-acting with a crazy person. I slow down, pretending I'm not horny as fuck or nervous around this woman behind me. Shrugging, I say, "Thanks for the drink."

"Anyti—"I slam the door closed and lock it. When I turn back, I go to her. "I ordered a drink for you."

I'm thanked with a smile before the words leave her mouth. Sultry. Salty-sweet lips. I want my mouth against hers again, staring at it when she says, "Thank you. That was nice."

There is absolutely nothing nice about my thoughts while watching her lips wrap around that straw and suck. "Fuck me."

Wide green eyes stare at me as I take her drink like I'm stealing candy from a kid. "What?" she asks before I realize I said *fuck me* out loud.

"No. Kiss me." I don't give her time to develop that sweet smile I know is going to crease her cheeks. I just fucking kiss her because it's all kinds of wrong that I wasn't kissing her already. My hands find her warm skin just under the hem of her shirt. As much as I want to slide farther up and take this dick tease of a T-shirt off her, that's not in the lesson plan today.

Fortunately kissing, all kinds of kissing, is. Our tongues embrace just as our bodies do. I move her slowly back, her knees halted by the loveseat. "Sit down," I say, keeping my voice low. When she does, I sit next to her. We take the moment to catch our breath.

"How am I doing?"

I shift in my jeans, the denim too tight and restraining for my erection. "You're an incredible kisser, but practice makes perfect." I lean over and kiss her. She leans back, fisting my shirt and bringing me with her. Lean legs spread and I take up residence. I could dry hump the hell out of her right now, but that's not on tonight's agenda.

Her mouth is warm and welcoming matching how I feel between her legs. Fuck. I push off the arm of the loveseat on either side of her head and sit back staring down at her. "You can't be like this."

Lifting up on her elbows, she looks confused. "Like what?"

"This." I wave my hand over her body. "No way you're still a virgin."

She laughs, and relaxes back, resting her hands behind her head. "I told you I've made out before. I'm not new to all of it. Just the final deed. But I'm out of practice. I haven't had a boyfriend since college. I've had dates, dates that were duds. I don't want dud dates. I want Lowry."All of me, everything from my lungs to my heart deflate under the mention of *his* name. Asshole. "What makes him so special? Trust me, V. You can get any guy you want. Why waste your energy and your virginity on him?"

"Because I can't get him."

"So it's a challenge, an ego thing?"

"No, not at all. I just want to be one of those girls that Lowry Renquist would be interested in." She sits up, her feet landing back on the floor. "Anyway, he might not be getting my virginity." She turns to me, a glimmer of hope reflecting in her eyes. "I was hoping that would be the final lesson with you."

"C'mere." She moves over and rests her head on my shoulder when I drape my arm around her. "I thought I was teaching you to get his attention."

Fingertips fidget with a button on my shirt before slipping just inside and scraping lightly with her nails. Big Richard reacts. *Naturally.* I take hold of her hand, stilling it. She looks up at me. "The women he dates are not virgins who fumble around the bedroom. They know how to please him." Her eyes lower, her gaze fixating on that button again. "I want to know how to please him."

I release her hand and lift her chin. When I see the sadness in her eyes, I say, "He doesn't deserve you. You know that, right?"

"I do. But I've been holding onto my virginity like it's a bargaining chip. It's not worth anything if I'm spending my life alone. I was always told not to settle, but I'm twenty-four and alone. Sure, I didn't settle but it came at the cost of not experiencing a real relationship at all. I don't want to be twenty-five and alone, so I'm willing to cash my chip in for the greater good. I want him to find me irresistible."

Her sadness seeps into me, hitting my heart. This is what men have done to her. "We're fucking jerks, Virginia. If they don't find value in you, you've got to find it in yourself."

"I'm not blind. I know on the outside I'm not the same girl in that photo, but on the inside, I'm still unsteady with this."

Eyeing her, admiring those perky tits she's so determined to unflatter under her business clothes. "So you hide it?"

She slides to the side, facing me while bending her leg

in front of her. "I can tell you don't like the suits, but that's what is expected of me at work. There's a dress code."

"Let me ask you something. This Lowry guy, has he hooked up with women in the office?"

"Yes," she says with an added nod.

"What are they wearing?"

"Oh God," she starts, an eye roll punctuating her feelings on the topic. "I don't even know how they walk in those skirts. They're so tight and their heels are ridiculously high."

"Two things—you said they as in plural. So he's fucking or has fucked several women in your office?"

She just nods this time. "Flirts with them, but not slept with any or at least the rumors say he hasn't."

"Secondly, why can they dress like that and you can't?"

"I'm in a different department. I'm the only woman in that department with six men. We wear suits."

"But it's not in the dress code officially." Narrowing my eyes as I follow my own breadcrumbs to my final point. "You're choosing to fit in with the men." Totally judging, I look at her with my lips off to the side.

I think she's starting to follow my thinking. She smiles and sighs. "I see what you're saying. It's me, not them. And not Lowry."

"Do you have a game plan? Are you just gonna show up to work one morning and jump him in the elevator or what?"

"New Year's Eve. Our company throws a holiday party on New Year's at the Waldorf-Astoria."

I feel sick to my stomach. "You want to kiss him at midnight on New Year's?"

Her excitement grows. "No, I want to seduce him at midnight on New Year's. Any advice?"

She's doing this no matter what I say, so I give her

honesty. "You have the power to get his attention, even though I still don't know why you want it. The bottom line is, you're not using your gifts."

"And by gifts, you mean?"

"Body. Those other women are giving him something to look at."

"I'm not using my body." She taps her chin. "Very good point, Hardy."

I hate leading a horse to water that's contaminated, but she's determined to drink from that trough no matter what I do. So that leaves me two choices: Help her win her man by giving her the skills to attract that asshole or let her fumble into his bed and give him a gift he doesn't deserve.

There really is no decision to be made. She trusts me. As much as I want to wisen her up on the ways of the world when it comes to men, I need to protect her more. If that means making love to her like she deserves, I guess I'm the luckiest bastard that ever lived.

Chapter Eleven

My hip is swatted, a towel cracking loudly against my jeans. A bird is flipped off to the side it came from before I even give the culprit a glance. "Fuck you, Clive."

While I continue to stare at Virginia, he asks, "How long are you going to ogle her? Cuz it's just past pathetic o'clock and heading toward creepy by my watch."

Looking down at the stainless steel Omega that shines on my wrist, I reply, "I've got a good ten minutes before I reach cat five creepiness."

"That's disastrous."

"And like you said, leaning toward pathetic."

"I said it's past pathetic."

I turn my back to her though it's against my better judgment to do so when that fucker in a Member's Only jacket is hanging on her every word and staring at her tits. And she's braless. Fuck me. My hands tighten around the knife I'm supposed to be using to cut oranges, my knuckles whitening under the pressure.

Being patted on the back, Clive says, "Those feelings will get ya every time."

"I'm not having feelings." Though I'm feeling I might kill this jackass in the jacket fawning all over her. One touch and he's going to lose a hand.

"Surrre you aren't." Clive reaches around and takes the knife from my hand. "I think it's safer if I take this away."

"For me or him?"

"Both." He laughs, and then nods toward Virginia. "You've known her for like what? A week?"

"Something like that."

"Wow. She must be really special for this insta-love you've got going on."

Scoffing, my head jerks back. "I'm not in love and there's no such thing as insta-love." *Is there?* I see Clive checking her out. "Hey, eyes over here."

He shakes his head. "See? I wasn't even looking at her and you've got your boxers all up your ass." Coming closer, he leans on the counter next to me and crosses his arms over his chest. "I'm not saying you're in love, but those two rules you live by when it comes to women . . ." His hands make an explosion hand gesture. "Have been obliterated."

"No way." I'm the one shaking my head this time, denial clearly setting in. I look back at Virginia. Her drink is empty, her tits perfect, and Members Only jackass has moved in. I'm there before he can offer her another drink. "Can I get you a refill?"

She smiles when she sees me; nothing like the expression of boredom she was giving that chump. "Thanks, Hardy. Maybe one more, but only if you can drink with me."

"I want to, but Eddie had to leave and I'm covering."

Checking her phone, she debates. "Maybe I should head home too. I have a long ride back and an ear—"

"Early morning?"

She laughs. "Yes, something like that."

When she gets off the stool, Members Only panics—a lot like I'm doing—and says, "Maybe we can hang out sometime? Or go for coffee?"

Her gaze hits mine. "Um . . ."

I step in. "Hey buddy, we're kind of seeing each other, so if you don't mind . . ."

Hands are up in surrender as he backs away. "Oh, man, sorry. I didn't know."

"It's new." I look back at her. "And going well."

He slaps a twenty down on the bar. "This should cover my drinks. Good luck to the both of you."

Virginia is laughing. "Thanks." When she turns back to me, she says, "Do I detect a hint of jealousy in your actions? Or just helping a girl out?"

"Maybe both. Definitely both."

Resting her elbows on the bar, she leans closer, and says, "I feel the same about you. That's how I know it's time to go. I know you don't want that line crossed and it's too easy for me to fall for your cute—"

"Ass?"

"I was going to say charms, but ass works too. When's our third lesson?"

"Saturday night?"

"Yes, it will almost be like having a date."

Yeah . . . almost. I sigh. "Your place or mine?"

She swings her coat around her and slips her arms inside. When she reaches for the zipper, Chopin's "Funeral March" begins playing as sadness consumes me watching the girls disappear. They were definitely a highlight of my night. "How about mine? If you're free all night we can have dinner out and then go back to mine for the lesson?"

"Sounds good. I'll text you with details."

Happiness covers her face. "I'm looking forward to it."

"So am I." I walk around to walk her out.

"I need to pay out."

"When you're here, I buy."

She nudges me in the side. "You know the way to a woman's heart."

Suddenly feeling like I don't know women at all, I just nod while looking down at my feet. "Yeah, I'm the expert." Except when it comes to her. We head for the door and I throw my arm out for a cab. She has her hands in her pockets. When a cab pulls to the curb, I signal one minute. Turning to Virginia, I lift her hood up, protecting her from the cold. The tip of her nose is already pink, so I kiss it. Any excuse really. "Be safe and text me when you get home. Okay?"

She nods. "I will." Moving closer, she lifts up and kisses my cheek. "Thank you for earlier."

"My pleasure." Literally.

"Have a good week."

"You too."

She dashes to the taxi and gets in the back. I do the universal sign for roll down the window to the driver like they actually hand crank down these days. I hand him plenty of money to cover her fare and his tip. "Take care of her and drive safely." Looking back at her, I feel sadness for a different reason other than her boobs being hidden from view, but I don't dare admit it. Instead, I cover, something I've gotten too good at doing lately. "When you're not around me, wear a bra. It draws unsavory attention from men when you don't."

She starts laughing. I know she sees right through me though she's nice enough to play along. "Okay, Hardy. Good night."

"Good night." I back away and watch the cab leave. This is becoming a habit I don't like. Her leaving.

Insta-love, whatever that is. It's a bunch of phooey is what it is. Watching her cab drive away, I think next time I'll ask her to stay.

***

By Thursday, I miss Virginia. We exchanged a few casual texts over the last few days—hi, hope your day is going well, sweet dreams, and that kind of thing. But then one night she sends my favorite: Thinking about you. Along with the text, she sends a photo of herself in a bubble bath. I can't see her face as the camera is facing the other direction. Look, I'm not saying she sent it to get a rise out of me, but I rise to the occasion no problem and jack off twice to that photo in two days.

I'm not embarrassed to admit that I did the deed with her photo next to me. I'm embarrassed that I did the deed with only her knee poking through the bubbles. That's it. One bare, wet, lustful, tempting and teasing kneecap. Damn that's a sexy photo. There might be something to this insta-love theory. Though I'm leaning more toward a chemical imbalance. Holding the bottle of pills up from five feet or so away, I ask the guy behind the register, "What do these do?"

"Hard dick. For hours." I should be offended by his bluntness, but the curly haired hipster seems to know his stuff. "It's a staff recommendation."

The little placard hangs from the shelf that displays the bottle. "Yeah, so I see." I set it back in its place. That's not what I need. If I could bottle the painful erections I've been dealing with, I'd be a millionaire . . . oh wait, I'm already a millionaire. Then I'd be a billionaire and market the hell out of those pills. Every bottle would come with that pic of Virginia's knee. Works for me. I'm sure it can work for others. This could bring groundbreaking advancements in men's penile projections. I don't even try not to laugh. I'm funny as shit.

After an hour of asking about almost every bottle of pills in the health store, I'm also starting to think that I'm out of luck with the chemical imbalance theory. "But Clive calls it insta-love. Is this really a thing?" I ask the hipster. I'd settled into a philosophical conversation on existentialist versus internalized love. He lost me on the self-love movement he was currently adhering to and inviting me to bear witness to the sanctity of it. I was brought back around when he mentioned love at first sight. His happened when he was three and "discovered" himself in the mirror. In reference to me, he claimed I was suffering from a clear case of socially acceptable attraction to someone I had physically bonded with resulting in a chemical change in my mind's matter. He reaches behind him and places a small box of Godiva's chocolates in front of me. "That will be nine eighty-seven."

"Why are you selling me chocolates?"

"Have you not been listening at all?" he asks, exasperated.

"I've been listening." Understanding is a whole other issue, but I've been listening.

"It's just love, man. You're overlooking the obvious. Just flat out, simple love."

Simple? Uncomplicated . . . "So I need chocolate to cure me?"

"There is no cure. Trust me, my friend. You're too far-gone. So you have to deal with the crisis at hand. Buy the chocolates and go see her. That's the closest to a prescription as you're going to get."

Go see her. I slap a ten bill down and take the chocolates, then tuck them into my coat pocket. "Keep the change."

"I was going to." The hipster opens the paperback in front of him back up and adds, "Good luck."

"Thanks. I'm going to need it." I walk out into the late afternoon and text Virginia. *What are you up to?*

She replies quickly, making me smile. *Just work, but off in forty, so YAY!*

I start down the street, but type: *Meet in the middle for drinks?*

Her: *Just tell me where and I'll be there.*

She doesn't have to tell me twice. I grab a cab and head for the city.

Forty-five minutes later I'm sitting at a table in the corner of a pub, waiting . . . correction: anxiously waiting for her to arrive. The bell chimes and a gust of wind ushers her inside. Despite the brown hair that was blown over her face, I know her. My heart beats erratically in response.

She pushes her hair back and looks around. When she spies me in the corner, Virginia smiles and life feels better because of it. I stand when she comes toward me. *Holy Jack Fucking Daniels.*

I step forward and as soon as she reaches the table, I take her in my arms and kiss her. Hard. With all the passion I've stocked up on since I last had my lips on hers. Breathless. I want to leave her breathless and wanting more. When our lips part, she languidly opens her eyes, and says, "I could get used to that."

"Never settle for less, V." I help her with her coat, but

put it back on her shoulders when I see what she's wearing. "Why are dressed like that?"

Laughing, she doesn't seem to be taking this matter as seriously as she should. When I start zipping her up again, she moves just out of reach while swatting my hands away. "What are you doing, Hardy?"

"You forgot your suit jacket at work. And from the looks of it, your bra as well."

"I took my bra off." She waggles her eyebrows and pulls a hot pink lacey strap from her purse. I push it back down just as quickly. Laughter rings out, the sound even making me smile. She says, "What are you doing? You said when I'm around you I don't have to wear a bra. I think they're uncomfortable so I took it off." After setting her bag on a chair, she takes her coat off again.

When she sits down, I sit down across from her. She adds, "Why are you looking at me like that?"

"Like what?" I ask, my eyes darting from her delicate collarbone that I bit and licked to the neck I'd love to mar with a hickey claiming her as mine for all to see, especially that asshole at her work. Claiming her? What the fuck am I doing?

Oh, the candy. I reach into my coat pocket and pull it out. Placing it on the table in front of her, I say, "I got you something."

"You brought me chocolate? Hardy?" she teases. "Be careful or I might fall in love with you." *Temptress.* "This is so sweet of you. Thank you."

"You're welcome."

"Want to share?"

"No, I want you to enjoy them in your bath."

She laughs freely. "I don't know why I sent that pic. Just being goofy."

"You can be goofy with me anytime."

The waitress comes to the table and we order two beers while I continue staring at her. My favorite pink, several shades lighter than this silky little top she's wearing, colors her cheeks. "You're making me paranoid. Do I look that bad?"

"No. You look amazing. I like this outfit on you. Shows off the goods."

That makes her laugh. "Well the goods got no love from Lowry this week. I think I'm going to have to practice lesson one on him."

Flirting? "No. If that outfit doesn't get his attention, flirting won't do jack shit."

"I noticed one of the personal assistants was wearing those red-soled shoes. What do you think about them?"

Christian Louboutin knows what a man finds sexy and seeing those red heels draped over your shoulders or at the base of long legs . . . "Don't waste your money. Guys don't care about that stuff." It almost pains me to lie to her this time. Her legs with those fuck me heels on would be an incredible sight to behold.

"Oh, okay. I just thought—"

"Well don't think about him. Like I said, he's not worth your time." My words are crushing, evidenced from the downfall of the corners of her mouth, but I can't seem to back this train up. Easy and uncomplicated have definitely vanished along with my patience.

"What's wrong, Hardy? You seem irritated."

"I'm fine." I drink some of my beer, insanely jealous of her efforts for this asshole lawyer. Looking her over again, was it me? Did I tell her to change the other day or is this her own doing? "What did the guys in your department think of your outfit?"

"Some didn't say anything. A few said I looked nice. Others hightailed to the bathroom every time they saw me. I ended up reapplying deodorant twice and spraying my perfume throughout the day they had me so paranoid that I stank."

Her innocence is revealed again and a belly laugh escapes me. "You're not smelly. Trust me on this." They're totally jerking off on the job. At least my work is in a bar. These horny sad sacks can't hold their shit together around her and they work in the Financial District.

She doesn't even realize how the world sees her. That makes me laugh harder, not in a laughing at her kind of way but that she has no clue that these guys are vomiting the snake because she's so hot.

Maybe I don't need to get all caught up in jealousy just yet. There's still a chance with her. As long as they keep seeing her as a geeky girl who's into numbers and dresses in boxy suits, I'm golden. That will give me enough time to make her see that I'm more than a shallow prick with divine sex skills. There's a guy and a heart behind this handsome mug. If only she'd take a good long hard look. She'd see I'm more than the parts that make me up.

I'm a whole man who has given up his life's creed to be with her.

Chapter Twelve

Once I laid down my emotional weapons and set aside my jealousy, I was enjoying my time with Virginia. Outside of Brooklyn—my place and the bar—I was seeing her in a new way. She is full of energy, hyped up on some copier incident at work, and moaning orgasmically over the best pastrami sandwich she's ever had. In case you are curious, it can be found at Katz's Deli according to her. I tell her I'll take her to Ben's Best back in Brooklyn. She'll never look back after that.

I'm hoping in more ways than one.

We order another round. She adds fish and chips. "All of this food talk has made me hungry."

I've been trying to figure out what it is about her that I'm falling so in . . . like, and lust with when it comes to her. "What do you like to do for fun?" I wink at her. "Other than spend time with me."

Reaching for a rubber band she has around her wrist, she takes it and pulls her hair into one of those knots hot chicks wear everywhere these days. I like her hair down, but with it looking so messy on top like she just woke up or maybe even had sex is kind of hot.

"Hardy? Helloooo."

Fast little hands waving frantically in front of my face bring me back to reality. Reality? Is this my new reality? Staring at a woman who clearly wants me sexually but wants nothing to do with me beyond that. Well, that's an exaggeration. She's here and our friendship is growing so I can't say *nothing* to do with me. She's just not reciprocating what I want with her seems closer to the truth. "Yeah?"

"You asked me what I like to do for fun. Did you not hear what I said?"

"Sorry." I rub my temples quickly before hunching down and giving her my complete attention. "What do you like to do?"

"I said," she starts, matching my body language, "you."

"Me what?"

"Are you really going to make me say it twice? It was hard enough the first time."

Hard. I almost say it but I'm losing my enthusiasm for the quick comebacks. *Am I losing my mojo?* Virginia slaps the table. "Oh my God, am I that boring?" She's laughing, but I can see the offense on her face.

"No. I'm sorry. I'm distracted today."

"I'd say so. What's on your mind? You can talk to me."

"Not about this."

Her mouth scrunches to the side. "Penis problems?"

Now I'm offended. "No. I don't have penis problems. Damn woman, go for the low blow why don't you?"

We both laugh and say, "Low blow." She adds, "Do you like that?"

The laughter lightens, and I reply, "A blow job? I'm a guy. Of course I like blow jobs."

"I tried to give a blow job—"

"Do I really want to hear about you blowing some guy?"

Sitting back, she's still full of giggles, and entirely too hot looking while doing it with her breasts bouncing against the silk of her shirt. "Oh come on. You're my teacher. If I can't talk to you, I have no one to get advice from."

"Don't you have girlfriends who like to talk about their conquests?"

"No." The laughter ceases altogether and I already miss the sound. "Other than Katie O'Dowd—"

I tap my glass on the table. "To Katie O'Dowd."

We clink our pints together and she continues, "My friends are just as helpless as me when it comes to finding love in the city."

"Maybe that's the problem. Maybe you're not meant to find love in Manhattan."

Her brow creases in the center, and she asks, "And where prey tell do you suggest I find it then?"

Brooklyn. Across the table from you. You're staring at him. "I don't know, but maybe love doesn't come in the form of Lowry Renquist, lawyer extraordinaire, but comes in the form of something more obvious, something right before your eyes but you're too blind to see."

"Speaking of low blows . . ."

"I'm sorry. I shouldn't have said that."

"I know how you feel about Lowry. You've been very sweet to me. You're looking out for my best interest and you make a valid point. I need to open my eyes and look around. There are plenty of other guys out there."

The food arrives, and she pushes the basket between us. "Wanna share?"

Everything with you. "Thanks."

Our time together is disappearing and when she stands,

I happily help her put her coat back on. She reaches for her bag and when she stands back up and turns, we're toe-to-toe. Resting her hands on my chest, she asks, "Why is it so easy with you?"

Easy? Interesting. The woman before me is anything but easy. "I've been thinking. What if—"

"Hardy Richard."

No. No. No. No. No. I know that voice. Too well. *No. No. No. No. No.* Please don't let it be her. Following Virginia's gaze, it's her and my heart sinks.

"Hardy. Yoohoo."

"Hello, Isabella."

With both her hands on my biceps, she comes in for the two-cheek kiss. I don't bother with either when our faces touch. Stepping back, she looks me over from head to toe and back again. "You're looking well. So casual in your flannel and jeans." Her voice is condescending, her remarks belittling dressed in fake appreciation.

With her target in sight, she sticks her hand out to Virginia. "I'm Isabella Collins, of Connecticut."

What the fuck is that about? "Shall I bow to thy royal highness?" Fuck this. I need to save Virginia and fast. "Actually, we were just leaving."

Virginia accepts the handshake, and replies, "I'm Virginia Ryan of Manhattan." Isabella looks down at my girl all bundled up and says, "A working girl."

"You make it sound so seedy, Isabella. On that note, we must be going." Reaching down, I grab my coat and take Virginia by the arm, whisking her away. Isabella remains standing where we left her, her mouth agape, and her hand on her hip.

"Call me, Hardy. We should get together."

I don't bother acknowledging her as we clear the door

and walk out into the cold night air. Putting my coat on, Virginia stands close, and says, "She was interesting."

"She's an ex."

"Girlfriend, fiancée, or wife?"

I hear the uptick in her tone, a tell tale sign. "Is that jealousy I hear, Ms. Ryan?"

She spins away from me, I'm sure rolling her eyes. "Not at all. You're allowed to have as many exes as you want." Looking back over her shoulder, she summons, and we start walking. "I'm sure there's a whole slew of women pining over the one who got away when it comes to you."

My face is too cold for big gestures. I shove my hands in my pockets, and laugh. "It's freezing."

"You realize you're not going to throw me off track that easily, right?" She bumps into me. "You always ask about me, but I want to know about you."

"How about coffee first?"

"Definitely coffee first."

We walk into a Starbucks and stand in line with the other freezing patrons looking for a quick warm up. "We met at college and continued dating after for a year." Dusting my hands together, I add, "That's about it." Trying to sidetrack her again, I ask, "Pastry?"

"Yes. Cranberry Bliss. It's my favorite and is only here for a limited time during winter." Without missing a beat, she says, "Now back up and let's go over how you ever dated someone so uppity."

Calling me on my shit. *Check.* I've got to hand it to her, she's good. Very good. "I wasn't always the laid-back handsome and extremely suave happy go lucky bartender you see before you. Oh wait, I've always been handsome and suave."

"And modest. I think that's what drew me to you."

If I weren't falling in love already, I'd be a goner for sure. "Yes, it's my 'modesty' that brings the bees to the honey."

"Ew, don't use animals or insects in reference to your penis."

I bump into her this time, and whisper, "Say it again."

"What? Penis?"

A little louder, I continue teasing, "Yes, Virginia, just like that."

She may be embarrassed, but her green eyes sparkle in the pastry counter lights. "Hardy," she scolds.

I can tell she likes it though, her smile becoming harder to restrain. "Yes, Virginia, you can touch my penis when we get home."

Frantically looking around to make sure no one heard me, she grabs me by the coat and squeezes the fabric. "Good lord, Hardy. What is wrong with you?"

"Yes, you're so bad it's good when you use the lord's name in vain."

"You are so going to hell." Not sure if I'm going to hell for real or if she's teasing, but either way, I like her feisty.

I slap her ass, the coat breaking the blow. "How about you take my name in vain instead? Will that get me into heaven?"

Loosening her grip, she lifts up on her toes, and whispers, "If I'm taking your name in vain, I promise you, you're already in heaven."

"Damn straight I am." I'll have to wait until I see the pearly gates. We have another lesson to learn before we get to the heaven that's awaiting me. I wrap my arm around her waist before she can escape and kiss her.

From the line, we hear the groaning, "Move up and get your coffee or get a room."

Virginia tucks her head against my chest, her emotions worn in the shade her cheeks turn. I lean back and tell the guy moaning behind me, "I'm working on both."She shakes her head, but at least she's still smiling. "Can we end the torture?"

"For you, anything." I kiss the top of her head right before she steps up and we order.

The small leather couch in the window by the Christmas tree is open and she beelines for it. We settle down, facing each other. She takes a sip of coffee, then asks, "What made you text me today?"

"I missed you." With my leg anchored on the cushion, I'm not even sure if she knows she's doing it, but her hand finds its way over, her fingertips rubbing back and forth. Dirty thoughts of those fingers rubbing something else come to mind. Grabbing her hand, I rest mine on hers. It feels so snug, though damn cold. "Geez, you're like an icicle."

That breaks any mushiness that was ballooning between us and we laugh. Pulling her hand back, she says, "Yeah, sorry about that. I need to buy a pair of gloves. I lost mine on the subway a week ago."

I take her hands back from her lap and placing them between mine, I gently rub, creating just enough friction to warm her up. And you're welcome. I set myself up with that usage of friction, but didn't go there like I could have. Holding my crude comments might be another side effect of the chemical imbalance Virginia causes in me. Though she might consider it a positive side effect, the guys would call me pussy-whipped. I wouldn't consider that such a negative though either.

When her hands feel warm, I release mine, and ask, "Better?"

"Much." Staring at me, she swallows hard and suddenly tension is present.

"What happened?"

"Why did you do that?"

"Warm your hands up?"

"Yes."

"Because they were cold."

With her coffee cup in hand, she turns to the window, shifting so her arm rests on the back of the sofa. Watching the snowfall, she says, "I love the snow, the quiet, the coziness of being inside, and building snowmen." When her gaze turns back to me, she looks sad. "People here are too busy to appreciate the joy in the simple things."

"I do."

"I'm discovering that's true. Is that the key to happiness?"

"Being content is the key to happiness. Appreciating what you have, instead of wishing you had more."

"You ever wanted what you can't have?"

Dragging the pad of my thumb over my bottom lip, I think about it. "Only once."

"What do you want that you can't have, Hardy?"

She hangs on every second as it spans between us, I look her straight in the eyes, and say, "It's bad luck to share your wishes."

The anticipation leaves her shoulders and she sinks against the couch. Letting her head roll to the side, she says, "I guess we should go."

Looking at my empty cup, I nod. "Yeah, I guess."

Out on the sidewalk, I ask, "How are you getting home?"

"Subway."

Looking at the time, it's almost ten. "I'd feel better if you took a cab."

"Are you worried about me, Mr. Richard?"

"I do worry about you. I also worry about your girls and why you refuse to give them the support they want."

"My boobs hate being trapped by that cruel underwire, so I think it's you who hates to see them carefree and happy."

"Trust me, there's nothing I hate about your breasts other than guys staring at them."

Grabbing her coat and pulling it tighter to her, she laughs. "No worrying about that in winter. Hey, before you leave, we're still on for Saturday?"

"I wouldn't miss it." I step closer, closing the gap. "I missed you."

Surprised by the turn in my tone, she looks up in curiosity. "You said that."

"I wanted you to remember it. I want it to be the first thing you think of when you think of tonight."

Her arms slide around my middle and she squeezes as my arms come around her, holding her close. She says, "I missed you too."

Our usual goodbye begins with getting her safely into a cab and sending her on her way. I grab a taxi to take me back to Brooklyn instead of waiting around watching her taillights disappear into the dark down the city street.

Right when I get comfortable in the back of a warm cab, I get a text from her: *I miss you already.*

Leaning back, I smile, then respond: *I miss you too, V.*

Chapter Thirteen

Saturday can't come soon enough. I know. This is not real. Virginia's made it more than clear that she wants another guy, but the next lesson is the one I've been waiting for. Well, besides the final lesson.

All sex aside, though I'll use my skills to the best of my ability, she said being with me was easy. I feel like I'm always finding my way back to that word. As much as I've been saying it's not easy being around her, it's just because I want her in ways that she doesn't want me. That makes it hard, literally all the time for me.

She's right though. It's easy to sit with her. It's easy to talk to her. It's easy to feel good around her. She makes me smile. She challenges me in ways that are unexpected—like the going without a bra thing. That befuddles me on a different level. It's like she's this vixen waiting to break free and has handed me the key to open the door.

Twenty-four hours until I put that key in the lock, but will it unleash her desires or set her free to be with another guy? It's a risk she's asked me to take without even realizing the risks involved.

Two lessons left to win her body.

Two lessons left to win her heart.

I will win the title, the grand prize, and all the blue ribbons. This is the Olympics of seduction, the final lap around the track. Do or die time. I'm determined to come out on top . . . or bottom, or from behind. I bet she'll like it from behind.

***

Friday night at The Hideaway is always busy. The hookups are happening early and the crowd is spirited. Three of us—Romeo, Clive, and myself—are covering the bar and Eddie's working the tables tonight—not something we usually do, but our bussing crew is late. Hiring more people is another thing on my never-ending list of things to do.

Cocktailing is fun. It's entertaining. It makes money. It's a skill that not everyone has. If they're reading recipes, they need to go back down to the minors. We're too busy to be looking up how much Angostura bitters goes in a Manhattan or white rum goes in a piña colada. Bartending is a profession and I expect my tenders to treat it as such. That is why I have low turnover. They are treated with respect and paid well. What they do on their breaks or how they get the customers back in the door is on them. As long as it's legal, I'm good.

Clive lays down a line of lemon drops for a group of friends on a girls' night. Romeo is down at the other end serving a group of guys out for a good time who are eyeing the girls. I hear him telling them to buy the ladies their drinks and then to introduce themselves before he has the pleasure. "Once they meet me, you have no chance."

His arrogance is well backed by years of having it reaffirmed. He's not called Romeo for nothing. His parents called it the minute they met him. The ladies have been falling for him ever since.

As for me, something's got to change. I need to spend less time working in the front or less in the back, but doing both is wearing me down. I think it's time to have a full-time manager come on board. Eddie's always been my right hand man without complaint. I'll meet with him soon to give him the news he's been working for.

I check on the far end of the bar where two women have been waiting longer than I like. "Sorry about the wait. What can I get you?"

I've seen the light haired brunette before. Somewhere, though I can't place it. Her lips are fire engine red and draw my attention. As her tongue dips out, she leans against the bar. Our eyes meet, hers looking me over before she asks, "What do you recommend?"

Normally I'd rattle off my standard for women with her hair—rum and coke, but I have a feeling she's not looking for that drink tonight. Her confidence exudes the bright lip color, so I take a guess, "Vodka martini?"

"Extra olives?"

"You got it."

Her friend wants the same, so I get to concocting their drinks. I overhear her friend talking to her about the latest episode of the reality show red-lips is on. That's where I've seen her. I'm not one to watch a lot of tele but I have a few guilty pleasures and trash TV at 3:30 a.m. is the perfect sedative after a long shift. I put five olives in each glass and then pour the liquid over the top. When I set the drinks down in front of them, red lips says, "Extra dirty. Just how I like it."

My feelings may be all mixed up after meeting Virginia, but I'm not dense. I know a come on when I hear it and just as I'm about to slip into my old lines now and maybe her later, I realize my mind is blank.

No lines.

No funny comebacks.

No sexual innuendoes.

Holy shit. *Am I broken?*

Two weeks ago I was happily chugging along minding my own business except when a pretty woman wanted me to mind hers. Now, PMV—post meeting Virginia—I'm standing in front a celebrity—although minor fame—she's gorgeous and hitting on me and I have no response other than, "Keep the tab open?"

Her expression falls. A credit card is handed to me, and she replies, "Thanks."

When I turn around and enter her card into the register, the women start talking to each other again, "I heard he was easy."

Easy?

There's that damn word again, but used in a way I never thought I'd hear in regard to me.

Red lips whispers, "I heard he was the best. I want the best."

"He doesn't seem interested."

Her huff is heard and I move to the other end of the bar. Tapping Clive on the shoulder, I say, "Take over the two at the end for me."

Leaning back, he glances down the long line of the bar, then back to me. With his eyebrow cocked, he asks, "You sure?"

"Yes. I'm sure."

While filling a pint glass, he keeps tabs on them. "What's wrong with them?"

"Nothing." I chuckle, restocking the wine glasses.

"But they're hot and you're tossing them to me?"

"They have their own minds, you know. I can't toss them to anyone. I'm just not interested."

"Why not?"

"Clive," I gripe. "Enough. Will you take care of them or not?"

"Sorry," he says, with his hands up. "I'll take over."

My annoyance has reached a peak, but I try to blow it off and calm down. "Thank you."

"It's almost sad to see it go, but I'm happy for you." He claps me on the back and takes someone's order.

I set another pitcher down for the guys at the end, and then add it to their tab. When Clive turns to ring up the drinks, I ask, "See what go?"

"Your pride. Your drive. The good times. We'll remember them fondly. You fought hard, my friend, but it's time to surrender."

"What the fuck are you talking about?"

"Rule number two."

"Pfft. Rule number two is firmly in place. Like stronger than ever. My feelings don't even dip into that lake, much less swim there."

"Would that be the lake of love? You sure you're not already skinny dipping with your heart on your sleeve?"

"Positive." Pretty sure. *Maybe*. Not at all. "Fuck." I walk out from behind the bar and head for the office. "Cover me, Eddie."

"Will do."

I don't turn on the light in the office when I enter. I like the dark. The little lights from technology are enough to find my way to my desk. Sitting down, I drop my head into my hands. When did it happen? When did I succumb to something I never gave any credence to? When did I fall?

It's not about when I fell, but how I catch myself. I dig my phone from my pocket and send a text to a friend.

The reservation is set at one of the best restaurants in New York City. It's good to have friends in the business. After confirming, I text Virginia: *Kat & Theo at 8?*

It's not what I wanted to type. I wanted to drop a whole confessional of sinful thoughts I'd had about her, thoughts that included that dreaded four-letter word. Not fuck though it's my favorite, but the one that starts with *L* and ends with an *E*. I didn't though because I may be falling apart at the seams, but I still have my dignity.

Lessons in love. That's all this is. Teach her so she can seduce the asshole from work. I bang my head against my wood desk. Then my phone dings with a message and I'm quick to look to see if it's her. It is! Success. I read: *I've always wanted to go there. See you then.*

See you then. I return the message a little too eagerly for my liking but what the hell. I had already blown my image of Mr. Cool the minute I agreed to her crazy plan.Setting my phone in front of me, I rub my hands over the scruff of my beard, then reach over and turn on the lamp. A knock comes too soon, and I say, "Come in."

Eddie peeks in. "The bussers showed up, so I'm back behind the bar. I brought in an extra bar back as well. He just got here."

"That's good. Hey Eddie, I've been meaning to talk to you. It's probably not a great time since we're busy, but I want you to think about moving into a manager position. Let me know your thoughts and we can discuss the details on Sunday when we both work."

Blinding white teeth are revealed when his smile grows. "Thanks, boss."

"Save the flirting for the ladies and get back out there."

"Will do."

The door shuts and as much as I want to spend more time moaning about my love life and the problems a cute little brunette has caused, I can't. It feels good to reward people who deserve it. *And really?* If life was that bad, I wouldn't have Virginia in my life at all, so I think I have it pretty damn good right now. Even if she is driving me mad.

I turn the lamp off, pocket my phone, straighten my vest and collar, and get back to work. It's not called Hardy's Hideaway for nothing.

***

What is this feeling?

I ran an extra two miles when I woke up today on what felt like pure adrenaline, but I do a few jumping jacks to shake this onslaught coursing my veins. When I stop, my breathing is harsher, but nope, still there.

In the bathroom, I take a closer look at my face. I've got color, so I stick out my tongue. Pink, like always. "Ahhhhh." Opening my mouth wide, I try to look at the back of my throat. Looks normal.

What's wrong with me? I haven't felt like this in years. Then, like a V-8, it hits me smack dab on the forehead. *Nerves.* More precisely, I'm nervous or anxious. I never did understand the difference, much to the contempt of my private school teachers. They swore to me I'd need to know this one day and here I am, using them interchangeably. They were right. Maybe I should track them down and let them know . . . What the fuck? Why am I rambling like this? Oh, the nerves. That's right.

Why am I nervous?

It's Virginia. Just lesson three. We've been here before. The first night we met I was touching her soft skin and causing those sweet heart-shaped lips to form that O from ecstasy. I can't wait to feel her heat and taste her desire again. I have absolutely no reason to be nervous. The last two lessons are my specialty. This is where I shine.

My skills in the bedroom are as good as my word. I always keep my promise and like The Hideaways motto— they always come, and always want to come back for more. That motto didn't invent itself. It came from years of experience and attention to detail. One taste and women were coming back in droves and bringing their friends. Look, I know what you're thinking. We aren't male prostitutes and we're not hooking up with everyone. The Hideaway is a place where women and men gather and meet. There's no pretension or judgment you find at a lot of the bars in Manhattan. So the clientele is hooking up with each other and we've had six marriages in the last two years.

For me personally, it's been a matter of that connection I spoke to Virginia about. A little human touch is good for the soul. I'm not screwing all of Brooklyn, but if I was, I still sleep like a baby at night. I'm okay with who I am. Well, I was . . . until Virginia and now I'm a mess.

I do twenty jumping jacks and fifty pushups before getting in the shower to help relieve some of the pressure aka nerves. Thinking about that sexy little kneecap does the trick. I never saw it the first time we were together, so this photo teases in the best of ways of all the body parts I've never seen that she's blessed with.

Extra time is spent getting ready as if this is a date. Virginia made it clear it was "almost like a date." Highly disappointing.

On top of the "almost like a date" comment, I'm sitting

here in my apartment completely dressed with nothing to do but worry about how this night and maybe the rest of the nights of my life are going to play out. Looking at the clock, it's only five thirty. Damn, what is wrong with me?

I can't sit here any longer. There are stops I need to make, so I grab my coat and gloves and head to the city.

Chapter Fourteen

The second I enter the shop he turns around and grabs a big box of Godiva chocolates and sets it on the counter next to the register. The health store hipster doesn't even look up. He just knows. Like he knew I'd be back. "I knew you'd be back."

See? He's intuitive like that.

"I need your advice."

When I reach the counter, he closes his romance novel with the pirates on the cover, and looks up. "The chocolate didn't work?"

"She liked it."

"All girls like chocolate. If she liked the other box, bring her more."

"I'm not sure chocolate will fix this mess."

After crossing his arms over his chest, he leans back and kicks his feet up on the counter. "Look, I'm no psychologist. I just know that we like to complicate things that aren't so complicated. Zen. We need to get Zen with our world, become one with the things we value."

"I'm trying, man. I'm just so fucking confused."

"Language."

"Huh?"

"Don't swear. Five years ago when I decided to find true harmony with the flowers and trees, swearing had to go. Except for roses. Those bitches love a foul mouth."

"What are you talking about?"

"Life. The journey we're all on to find peace in our existence. You're what? Like forty?"

Really? "Twenty-eight."

"Whoa! Your aura is a tangled mess."

"I know. That's why I'm here."

"You're here for chocolates. You may not have known that when you walked in, but this box," he says, pushing it forward, "will lead you to what you need."

"A box of chocolates?"

"Trust me." When I pick up the box, he adds, "That will be twenty-tree ninety-five."

"For chocolates?"

"There's a lot more in this box than the last."

"Whatever. Here you go and keep the change."

"Thanks, man, and I work on Monday if you want to do a recap of your date."

"How did you know I had a date?"

"Really?" He points at my clothes.

"Fine." I turn for the door. "I'll see you on Monday."

"After twelve. I like to sleep in."

I roll my eyes and head back out the door. With my arm in the air, I have one more stop to make before I meet Virginia, so I hail a cab. When I get in, I say, "Bendel's please."

He eyes me in the rearview mirror, and then nods. "Fifth Avenue. You got it."

I walk into the store, and two ladies chatting straighten

up and smile. "Can I help you?" They both ask at the same time before quick stepping around a display until they're standing next to each other with large grins. One of their mouths tenses and she nudges the other. "My turn."

The other one huffs and backs away. The saleswoman approaches and this time speaks in a softer tone. "How may I assist you, sir?"

I might be mistaken but when she says sir it sounds like a purr. I like it. A lot. "I need a gift."

"For your girlfriend or wife?" I swear she bats her eyelashes at me.

But I'm too busy trying to figure out what Virginia is to me to pay much attention. "Umm . . . a friend. A lady friend. A woman friend."

"Lovely. I see you have Godiva Chocolates. So you're looking for something else for a birthday orrrrr?"

Damn, all of these questions were unexpected. "A gift because she doesn't have any."

"Any?"

"Gloves. She lost hers. So I want to get her a new pair of gloves."

"Right this way, sir." While we walk from this area with the handbags displayed into another with scarves and hats, she asks, "Gloves are a very thoughtful gift for a friend, but no occasion?"

I start saying it before I can stop myself, "Third base."

The saleswoman does a double take. "Well in that case, I suggest cashmere. Unless you're planning on turning third base into some bondage in the bedroom, and then I suggest my personal favorite—leather. Either way, both are nice"

A million excuses for my lewd behavior cross my mind, but nothing is going to take away the humiliation I feel. So I just carry on like my chemical imbalance isn't controlling my mouth since she seems to suffer from the same disorder. "Cashmere sounds great."

When we reach an empty counter, she says, "Well this is odd. Let me check with Regina."

"Okay." I stand there awkwardly holding my box of chocolate, but then I spot a pair hanging on a display near the front window. I make my way past two older ladies who are contemplating the life cycle of bees and using buzzing sounds to back their point. I whip around an oval table, and just as I reach the display with a mannequin atop, another lady swoops in and grabs the gloves. "I was going to get those."

Taken aback, the lady, about my mother's age, says, "So am I."

My original saleswoman and Regina—the glove manager or would it be manager of gloves—anyway, they intervene. And when I say intervene, I mean, offer to wrap the gloves for the lady who stole them out from under me. "Wait," I say, "do you have any other pairs? Any color. Doesn't matter."

Regina responds too calmly to be trusted. "No, sir. That was our last pair. Christmas is only a week away and gloves and winter go together like, well, like gloves in winter."

Checking my watch, I only have forty-five minutes to get to the Flatiron District, which seems nearly impossible to do with the snow and this lady holding onto the gloves like I'm going to steal them. I decide to plead my case. "I really need those gloves. I'm begging you. I want to give them to a woman I'm meeting at a romantic restaurant in hopes to win her heart." *Wait, what?* Is that what I'm doing? Oh shit. I just might be. "I got these chocolates and I'm sliding into third base with her tonight, but she lost her gloves and she has really great hands—pretty fingers that she likes to use to express herself when she talks. Solid grip —oh wait, I probably shouldn't go into all the details. My point is, I want to protect them and keep her warm."

The three ladies are staring at me with that look—it's the one of love that I see at the bar. I think they're going to help me out when the customer with the gloves in her hands says, "I love chocolate."

I'm not sure what my face is saying, but she taps the box in my hands.

Dot.

Dot.

Connect.

"Ohh. You like chocolate. Do you like Godiva?"

"I love Godiva."

"How about a trade?"

"Done." I hand her the chocolates and she snatches them from me like I'm going to tease her and take it back.

The soft fabric of the gloves is securely in my hands when Regina says, "Let's go ring you up."

As the woman digs into the candy box, I realize the health store hipster was right. This box of chocolates led me to what I needed. Wow. My mind is kind of blown right now. I buy the gloves and shove them in my pocket before grabbing a cab to the restaurant.

I'm late. I hate being late, but I especially did not want to be late tonight. Fortunately, Virginia is later. I'm led to our light green booth toward the back of the restaurant and seated. It's rude to order a cocktail before the other guest has arrived, but the nerves from earlier have flocked back like seagulls on a bad hair day. That doesn't even make sense to me. I'm convinced I'm officially broken because I met a virgin named Virginia who made me break my own rules before I had a say in the matter.

All the chaotic thoughts and worries about having a jokeless future vanish the moment I see her. I stand beside the booth and watch her come to me with a walk that catches every guy's eyes in the joint. Holy shit.

Her hair is wavy-curly, hanging down past her shoulders the way I like it best. She's got heavier eye makeup and lighter lips. The red dress hugs every curve and the thin straps highlight the beauty of her neck and shoulders. My eyes go low and *damnnnn*, she's wearing shiny black heels that beg to be wrapped over my shoulders.

My heart starts racing the second I see her smile, the smile that she's wearing just for me. I step forward just as she reaches the table. Kissing her on her cheek, I whisper, "You are the most magnificent woman I've ever seen."

Keeping my cheek against hers, my hand runs along the curve of her waist. I want her. I want this woman more than anything I've ever wanted—not just sexually, but in my life, every day. Every morning. Every night. In my bed and in my heart.

Her hands are wrapped around my back, and she whispers, "You look incredibly handsome, Hardy."

"Maybe we should skip dinner?"

"No," she replies, laughing. "I've wanted to eat here since it opened but it was too hard to get into. How'd you get a reservation on such short notice."

"Magic."

"And by magic, you mean connections?"

"Exactly."

"Hardy?"

"Yes?"

She starts to squirm. "Are we going to stop hugging long enough to have dinner?"

"Do you want to? I'm totally fine standing here holding you like this all night."

Laughing, she whispers, "We can do this again when we get to my apartment if you like."

"I would like to do that." I release her and lean back. Her sweet smile pierces my heart. My hand gravitates to my chest and I rub.

She winks at me. "I've been looking forward to this lesson since the first time we were in your office."

"You have?" I take her jacket and purse from her arm and slip them into the booth between us as we slide in on opposite sides. She instantly moves them to the side and scoots closer to me.

I don't even think she's aware how close she's sitting until the waiter comes by and tells us what a beautiful couple we are. She puts a few inches between us and though I'd love to make a joke about ten inches I'd like to put somewhere, I'm too busy trying to find a reason to close the distance again.

We order wine and sit back, in no rush to order food despite being starved. I want my time with her to last as long as it can. "How was your day?" I ask.

"I cleaned and did some shopping. I got this dress today and these shoes. I treated myself. Ever since you talked about how the other women dressed around Lowry, nothing in my wardrobe made me feel good."

"Does this dress?"

"Yes. I feel pretty and in these heels, I feel tall. I like feeling powerful like that."

"A woman who carries herself with confidence is extremely sexy."

"So maybe I'm not a lost cause after all."

Our bottle of wine is opened and we take the time to

test it. The pinot noir reminds me of her lipstick the first time I ever saw her. I've been craving this wine ever since. "Salut," I say, holding my glass to hers.

"Salut."

Conversation flows throughout dinner and I learn that she loves golf and yoga, but hates horseback riding because she was thrown once, and she's willing to jog with me, but fears she won't be able to keep up.

She loves the snow. She loves when it rains. She hates when they mix. She has annual memberships to The New York Botanical Gardens in the Bronx and The Met and often frequents the New York City Library, but rarely goes in.

"Why don't you go in?" I ask, turning the stem of my wine glass between my fingers.

"Because it hurts my heart to leave." She tilts her head down, almost embarrassed by her admission. When she looks back up, she whispers, "It's just too beautiful to be real."

My hand stops and my eyes fix on her. She asks me, "Have you ever seen something so beautiful that it takes your breath away? Tasted something so amazing that you almost can't eat it, read a book that was so incredibly written that you're swept away in a fictional world and never want it to end?"

"I have," I confess instantly. I have. *You, Virginia.* You.

"I also love tacos." Her head rolls back in delicious ecstasy and I can't wait for it to roll back when I eat hers. "I can eat them for breakfast, lunch, and dinner." By the happy glint in her eyes, I believe her.

Our first course arrives and though the portions are small, they are artfully presented. Throughout dinner, our knees knock together. Nothing is said about it. Between friends or anyone else, it wouldn't be a big deal at all but to me, it's everything.

The predicament I've found myself in is quite funny if I could step outside of being an insider to this train wreck that has become my love life. Physically, I can have this gorgeous woman any way I want her. She's open and receptive. She trusts me with her life, her sex life at least. Emotionally though, we're a mess of the calamitous variety.

Does she not see how I look at her? No, putting it plain and simple. She doesn't see how the world sees her so how could she think anyone would see her any different. Fate played her hand when she brought Virginia Ryan into my bar, and right into my life. Now it's up to me to decide how we end. It's time to up the ante and raise the stakes. And I know just how to do that. "Want to play?"

"Play what?" Taking her hand in mine, I bring it down under the table. She's quick to catch on. "You want to practice?"

"Yes."

"Okay," she says. Her voice is tentative and filled with the nerves I shed once I saw her. She glances around the room quickly and then turns back. She knows my next move, and she relinquishes her reservations. Letting me guide her, she asks, "Show me what you like?" When I rub her palm over my cock, my name comes at the top of a deep inhale, "Hardy."

Moving her hair behind her shoulder, I kiss her neck, then whisper, "Yes, Virginia?"

A gulp follows and she looks at her wine. Her voice is low, timid, but her curiosity is eager like her hand as she grips me, getting a good feel. "You're so hard." When she finally dares to look in my eyes, she asks, "Was the appetizer an aphrodisiac?"

"No." My voice is clear. My eyes are focused on the beautiful woman who has completely enchanted me. "You're my aphrodisiac, V."

"Be careful," she says, a small smile gracing her stunning features. "When you say things like that I might believe you."

"Believe me, you turn me on so much it's hard not to drop you down right here in the middle of this restaurant and not have my wicked way with you."

"Is dropping me down what you really want?"

"No," I answer honestly as I lean back wrapping my arm around her shoulder as she gets more than a handful.

"What do you really want, Hardy? Tell me. Show me." She stops rubbing and squeezes, getting a firm, controlling hold on me.

I cover her hand again and guide her like she requested. "If I could have anything right now, I'd have your lips wrapped around my dick. I want to feel the back of your throat with the tip and have you swallow just to feel the embrace."

Her chest is rising and falling, a pale pink blossoming as her fingers drag slowly over her skin. "Hardy?"

It's getting stuffier in here, my body heated from her teasing. "What, sweetheart?"

"I want that too."

"Check!"

Chapter Fifteen

Lesson Three: Aptly named—Third Base.

"So what does third base entail?" Virginia asks on the cab ride from the restaurant.

"What we did the first night we met. That was third base." I don't tell her how much I've missed touching her intimately, possessively, and with a purpose—to get her off, which gets me off.

"I've missed that." A sigh that's reminiscent of a girl that has loved before whisks from her lips.

"You missed making out?"

"I've missed making out with you."

I lean over and kiss her because damn she just can't say things like that without expecting me to touch her in some way. Call me a greedy bastard. *What can I say?* It's been too long since I've been with a woman.

Actually it's been weeks, ever since this amazing woman walked into The Hideaway. I feel like I should send her a condolence bouquet now. Hell knows I'm going to need all the strength I can gather to not act like a baby whale discovering it's blowhole for the first time.

Damn bro. I shake my head at myself. I'm so broken. My humor falls flat at my feet. Even I'm not entertained by my usually amusing self. Maybe tonight will heal both me and my quick wit.

She says, "I love kissing you."

"I love . . ." Eh, eh, eh. I'm not going there. She smiles as if she knows the slip that almost slid right out of my mouth.

I pay the driver and we get out in front of a modern building surrounded by other more contemporary architecture.

"We're here."

"I sort of had you pegged for a brownstone walkup kind of girl."

She twirls in front of me, the wine going to her head and freeing her spirit. "I like keeping you guessing." "That you do, my dear. That you do." The door is opened for us, and we walk in. "I can appreciate the modernist approach to real estate and the boom in condos that are sleek with clean lines." What I won't go into with her is that this building is so similar to the one I used to live in. Once I left the hustle and bustle of the city I needed to change everything and that's when I bought my building. It was dilapidated and almost condemned for the missing windows and doors. Four stories of character and old Brooklyn history were almost demolished. I made the city a deal they couldn't refuse and took on the project with my contractor who was working on my bar. After one and a half years of renovations, the first three floors of apartments were done. The fourth floor—my future residence should be done within the next month if the weather cooperates.

The full floor with private elevator and an entire rooftop terrace will be all mine. Years of hard work and dreams have been sunk into my business and building a better life than I once had. I can appreciate her building with the doorman and amenities, but I don't miss this lifestyle.

She takes my hand and we walk through the brightly lit lobby to the stainless steel elevators. Virginia said hello to the doorman when she passed and wished the lobby clerk a good evening. It's little things like that, small gestures that say more about the kind of person she is than the louder ploys for attention she thinks she needs to attract the asshole.

The elevator doors open and I swing her inside and pin her to the wall. "How are you still single, Ms. Ryan?"

"You tell me, Mr. Richard." She glances to the buttons and says, "Twenty-three."

I hit the button and when the doors close, I run my nose along her neck, taking in her scent. "You're beautiful but stubborn, intelligent but with the tiniest bit of naivety. You're strong and defiant, sexy, and demure." Touching her lips, I lean in and kiss the corners. "You are a siren wearing an angel's halo. What am I going to do with you?"

She's almost breathless, but her hand slides around my neck, and says, "Anything you want."

My mouth covers hers and our lips part, our tongues engaging. Bending down just enough to find the hem of her dress under her coat, I start slowly, methodically dragging the fabric up with my hand. "I'm going to eat your p—"

The elevator dings and the doors open. We both release a breath as the tension escapes the elevator and we walk off hand in hand. She says, "Hold that thought."

"I'll do more than hold it, babe."

"That's what I'm counting on, professor."

"Professor? I like that." She leads me down a corridor

and around a turn. Her apartment is at the end. The key unlocks it and I hold the door while she enters first.

"My Professor of Romance."

My eyebrows waggle and I run the palm of my hand over the round of her ass. "I had no intentions of romancing you tonight."

"Want to come inside?"

"Do I ever?"

This time she breaks character and laughs. "You really do have a talent for the sexual innuendoes."

"I've listed it as a skill on my résumé." The view is great. The city is lit up just outside the large living room windows, reminding me so much of my past.

"I bet you did. Drink? I have a great pinot noir."

Running my hands through my hair, I can feel my veins twisting to find some of my old self inside. I'm not sure if I should give in or block the feelings from resurfacing. Gentle. I want to be gentle with her and if I let the past seep back in I might not be. "Do you have whiskey?"

She hangs her coat and bag on some hooks by the door. "I bought a bottle of Jack Daniels. I wanted you to feel at home."

I do. *Too much in this environment.* "Thanks."

"You're the cocktail expert, but can I make it for you?"

"Yes. Thank you," I reply, looking over at her in the kitchen. "I like mine neat."

"Is that without ice?"

"Yes." I walk to the large window. It's not floor to ceiling like mine, and her apartment is a lot warmer. It has a very Virginia feel throughout. Music starts to play, Frank Sinatra singing Christmas carols. I always preferred Dean Martin, myself. He never kowtowed to the establishment. Ol' Blue

Eyes was good, and damn talented, but Dean held his own while holding a martini in the other hand.

Virginia stands next to me, keeping her eyes forward. "I rented it for the view." She turns to me. When I look at her, she hands me my drink. "And it's close to work."

"Do you like what you do?" I take a heavy sip and watch her over my glass. Her smile is one I've seen a million times when patrons at the bar are asked the same question. It's what they do, not who they are. It's another reason the bar does so well. They can shed their responsibility and just have a good time.

"I like numbers. I'm that geek who can get lost in the combinatorics of Euler's equation all afternoon."

"Yet you picked The Met Fifth Avenue instead of Breuer."

"I love the geometry of contemporary art, but I find beauty in the ages of art and how it was depicted through the different cultures. Anyway, it's good to see things outside of your comfort zone."

"Have you ever been pressed against a window, exposed in ways that leave your soul bare like your body and kissed with so much passion that you can't and won't constrain it to only your lips?"

Her mouth is open, her breath deepening. "Good God. Warn a girl." She's fanning herself with her hand and turns to look back out the window.

"Answer me."

From my tone, my expression, she understands the gravity of my question. "No, Hardy. I haven't. Have you?"

"No, but I want to. I want to take you to that place where you forget that others might see and begin to crave that they do. And if they have never experienced the edge of that blissful abyss, they get a glimpse into what true ecstasy can be."

Her body is closer, her chest heaving. I can hear her breath. I witness the way she licks her lips. Resting my hand over her heart, I feel the pounding—begging for more. She whispers, "I want that."

"How badly?"

"Enough to know I'm ready for lesson four."

Moving my hand to her cheek, I say, "No, you're not, but you're ready for me and lesson three."

I take her drink and mine and set them down on the windowsill. "Do you remember what we did in the office?"

"Everything. I think about it all the time."

Smiling, I take her left hand in mine and put my other on the curve of her waist. "Dance with me again."

Her silent permission is enough for us to start moving, our bodies pressed together, and her head leans on my chest. I wrap my arms around her and we sway. Rubbing her back, I close my eyes and appreciate that I've been given a chance to hold her.

And to kiss her like this. Leaning back, I find her chin and turn it up to mine. "I want you," I whisper, and then kiss her, her lips taking to mine as if they should never be apart.

They shouldn't. That's a conversation for another day. Lesson three awaits . . .

Letting my hands roam as if she was mine, I grab her ass and squeeze her against me, enough so she can feel how she affects me. Her body starts moving of its own accord. "You want this. I can feel it. I can tell. Your body gives you away. Where's your mind?"

"On you."

"Good, baby. So good." I take a step back. "Sit on the sill."

"There?" She points to the windowsill behind her. It looks to be wide, like eight inches or so.

"Yes, Virginia. There."

She holds my gaze for a hard moment before she backs up and sits next to our drinks.

Keeping my voice steady, I use my experience to show her a new side of sex, one where she doesn't have to feel unsteady about the next step. She can just sit back and enjoy. The pleasure will truly be mine. "I'm thirsty."

Lifting the glass of whiskey next to her, she starts to raise it but detours and with the little vixen's eyes on me, she takes a long pull of the amber liquid. No scrunched face in reaction from the strength of alcohol. No, not her. She takes it like she loves it, keeping her eyes on me the whole time in challenge. Then her tongue dips out to lick her lips as she hands the glass to me.

My tongue dips in response, wishing I were licking her lips instead of mine. I take the glass from her and drink, finishing it. Reaching forward I set the glass back down on the sill and hold her head, angling it up to me. I kiss her lips, too tempted to stay away. Our lips part and our tongues pick up dancing where our bodies left off. When a little moan is given from her to me, my right hand moves down over her soft skin and I run a fingertip under the top of her dress. "You're so beautiful."

"You always say that," she whispers. With a shaky smile, she touches my neck, her fingers curving around holding me close to her. "You know I'm a sure thing, right? It's part of the whole plan."

Plan . . . the damn plan. "I say it because I think it and because you deserve to hear it." I'm going to make her forget all about that fucking plan. Kneeling before her, I slide my palms over her knees, her sexy little knees, and part them. They don't go far until I start to slide the skirt of her dress higher on her outer thighs.

Breathy with stiff arms holding her in place, she tugs that bottom lip under with her teeth. "I'm going to make you feel so good, V."

With my eyes latched on hers, I slide my hand up her inner thigh until I reach her paradise, a private haven where she greets me with my name sounding closer to a sin than the moniker my family intended. "Hardy."

My smirk is fast and quick, opposite of how I plan on touching her. "What is it? What do you want, baby? Tell me."

Her eyes leave mine when she turns her head to the side, dipping it down in a gesture that comes in the form of an unhealthy helping of disgrace.

I'm just not going to have that. "Look at me." My hand stops, although still warm against her softness. "Now." When she does look at me, I say, "Clear your head. There's nothing to be embarrassed about between us. Don't let demons in that have no place here." I rub her temple. "Or here." Moving my hand to her chest over her heart, I tap. "Or even here." I move my other hand, lovingly, gently, caressing her soft folds with the back of my fingers. "All of you—mind, body, and heart—have to want this, need to feel pleasure instead of shame."

"This is why I'm still a virgin. If one thing was out of sync and I let any negativity or fear in, it grew."

"You're not going to do that with me. You know why?"

"Why?"

"Because you know I'm here for you. You can slow this

down. You can tell me to stop, and I will. Anything you want, I want." "I've been called a tease."

"This is about you overcoming the girl you were in the past and embracing the woman you are now. The woman who lives without regret or fear, who owns her sexuality and who takes what she wants just for the pleasure in it." I find her clit, her body responding, I ask, "So tell me, Virginia, what do you want?"

"That." Her answer is pointed. Her eyes full of the lust I feel for her.

"Do you want my hand or do you want my mouth on you?" Her body responds, my hand wet with her desire, and I glide my tongue over my bottom lip waiting for her answer.

Fighting her shyness, her reserved nature when it comes to sex, she takes a deep breath, closes her eyes, and leans her head against the glass, letting her body relax under my touch. "I want your mouth on me, Hardy."

"Where? Tell me where you want me."

"I want your mouth on my pussy."

Green eyes look into mine and she finds that moxie that usually only comes out when she's feeling sassy. "Take off my panties, Hardy." My smile is wide and I'm more than happy to assist in getting her naked. Taking them by the lace I slip them down her thighs and over her calves.

Black patent. Red soles. High as the fucking sky heels. Fucking shoes. Literally. Even if I get her completely naked, these shoes are going to stay on. She leans back against the glass of the window and I make my move. Lowering my body, I take her legs one at a time and put them over my shoulders until she's straddling me. "Do you know how fucking sexy you look with your legs wrapped around my neck like this?"

"So are you. So very handsome and sexy kneeling between my legs."

Holy Jack Fucking Daniels! Hearing her call me sexy is hot as Hades. Her fingers slide into my hair and now I pass the power and let her take control.

Chapter Sixteen

My tongue dips first, the first taste savored. My breath pushed from my lungs, as she becomes the only air I need. Her body is open for me, radiant with want, with her desire for me. I flatten my tongue and cover her solidly. Her nails scrape lightly over my scalp as I build her tension, my cock stirring and hardening in the process.

Her little moans grow louder while I eat her. When I add two fingers to fuck her, I suck on her clit until she can't sit still. Minutes. It only takes her a few minutes before her pussy clenches and her clit is pulsing.

My dick is straining, the ache growing impossibly hard. Needing to find something to help relieve the pressure, I lick my fingers and stand before her. My desire is evident on more than just my face. Her eyes focus as her orgasm subsides. She reaches for my belt, and says, "Come here."

Taking two steps closer, I watch as she undoes my belt and then the button and finally the zipper. She reaches into my pants. "Underwear, Mr. Richard? I thought you were the commando type."

"I needed to wear something since I'd be around you. If not, I might be tenting so much wood that I'd get arrested for public indecency."

Her palm is warm, her grip too light. I cover her hand, making her grasp it more firmly. She smiles. "Public indecency sounds so hot. You're such a bad boy."

"Maybe you should punish me, with your mouth."

"Maybe I will." Big Richard is left alone, but then he's freed and his weeping tear licked right off. Her tongue tastes, and when her gaze reaches mine, he twitches. "Do you like that?"

"Yes."

"Tell me what you want me to do, Hardy? Do you want me to take your big, smooth cock into my mouth? Do you want to see my lips wrapped around you, sucking you so hard you forget your name until I call it out when you're fucking me with your fingers again? Or do you want to fuck my mouth? Tell me. Tell me what you want and you can have it. You can have me however you want me."

"Fucking hell, Virginia. Open that dirty mouth of yours. I want to see those pretty lips wrapped around me so badly."

"How badly?"

"I've gotten off to that image more times than I can say five finger Freddy while sober."

A smile returns to her face. "Then we shouldn't waste any time."

Fingers take hold of me and she leans down, taking me between her lips with purpose. My head drops back, the sensation overwhelming me. "Oh fuck, Virginia." *Heaven.* This is fucking heaven on earth. But I don't want to miss a second of this visual. I'll use the material another day when the most gorgeous woman I've ever laid eyes doesn't have my dick in her mouth. She moans and I just about blow. Fuck. I'm not going to last long.

Then she does this magical swirling thing with a suck and a pop at the end and slides back down my cock, sending me to the back of her throat. Like the queen of the unicorns she is. I grab the back of her head, needing to hold onto something while she swallows around me. "God damn." She stays in place until I say, "Hey."

She looks up, her lipstick smeared like I had fantasies about the first time I ever saw her. Bending down, I kiss her cheek. "You're amazing. You know that?" A little shake of her head shows me she doesn't know and that's just unacceptable. "You are."

"I appreciate that, Hardy, but I know you're just saying that."

"I'm saying it because I mean it. Like I said before, it's not just a physical thing. Chemistry and seduction take heart, soul, your thoughts in the right head space. All of those factors matter. Sex is science and math—all the key components play a part or it falls apart."

I kiss her on the lips. "So your beautiful brain works great but you need that sweet heart of yours to catch up with your body. Follow your instincts. They won't lead you wrong."

Putting her arms around my neck, she smiles and it feels so good to see. "Thank you. I don't deserve you."

"You're right. You deserve better than me, but I'm the bastard you propositioned, so I'm here by default."

I stand up and help her to her feet. Bending down again, I slide her dress back down over her hips. When I stand up, a pretty blush colors her cheeks. "We just gave the neighbors quite a show."

"Good. If they're too busy watching us, then they probably need the free show." Holding her by the arms, I can tell her legs are still a little unsteady from bending like she was. "Hold onto my shoulder." I seriously fucking love how much she trusts me. She doesn't ask a million questions. She just rests her hand on my shoulder. I bend and take one of her legs by the ankle and lift. I take that shoe off and she lands with her foot flat on the floor when I reach for the other. I repeat the same thing before standing up.

With hearts in her eyes, she says, "That has to be one of the most erotic things I've ever experienced." A giggle follows.

"That's saying a lot after what we just did."

"It's saying everything. Thank you, Hardy."

"You're welcome."

She takes a deep breath and releases it revealing a smile. "I'm going to change clothes. Help yourself to more whiskey if you want it."

I watch as she walks away, never tiring of the view of that great ass. When she disappears into her bedroom, I go into the kitchen and refill my glass.

Calling from the other room, she says, "Hardy?"

"Yeah?"

"Can you help me with this zipper?"

I have the glass to my lips, but when she calls, I go. She tastes better than whiskey ever will. When I reach the doorway, I look in. Her bedroom is so her—stylish and welcoming. She has what has to be the fluffiest comforter I've ever seen draped over the bed. I want to dive in, but she's standing next to it and wow, my breath is lost to the vision of her in red again.

Yeah. Yeah. I know I just had her in ways that are intimate and special, but it's like the reminder is there, making me want to skip ahead to lesson four right now. I walk to her and move her hair over one shoulder. Taking the zipper pull in hand, I slowly unzip it, appreciating every inch of skin exposed, and letting my fingers run the length of her spine. "You look incredible in this dress."

"I'm glad you like it. I bought it for the holiday party. It's Herve Leger. I splurged."

My hand stops as my gaze rises to the back of her exposed neck, the same neck I like to kiss, lick, and suck. She keeps talking, not noticing that I'm frozen to the spot trying to control this pain in my chest . . . these feelings. Fuck. "Between the shoes and the dress, I spent a month's worth of rent, but you seem to like them so I'm hoping it's money well spent. I'm really hoping to make an impression on New Year's."

"You bought this for him?"

She glances back at me over her shoulder. "I bought it for the party."

"You bought this dress for that asshole, but wore it for me for what reason?" I spin her around to face me, holding her by the upper arms. "To see if it would get the reaction you're hoping to get from him?" Her gaze falls from mine as shame takes over. "Look at me, V. Look at me and tell me the truth."

"Well yes," she says, hesitantly. "I knew if you liked it on me, Lowry would like it."

My hands fall away and I raise my head, my gaze searching her ceiling as I try to calm the turmoil that's spinning inside of me. When I look back at her, I see the anxiety return to her eyes, the same I saw the first time she apologized to me. And as much as I want to calm it, I don't. I won't. She needs to feel it. She needs to feel what it's like to hurt someone who cares about her, so she doesn't do it again. I bite my tongue and move around to unzip the dress the rest of the way. Then I walk out of the bedroom and straight for the kitchen. I'm staring down at the glass of whiskey when, from a distance behind me, she says, "Hardy, I'm sorry. I wasn't thinking."

I don't turn around. I don't let her off. I just take the glass and finish the liquor. When I set it down on the counter, I close my eyes, and drop my head. "When are you going to see, Virginia?" Disappointment, heartbreak, and resolve fill my tone, and I say, "This won't be pretty."

"What?" There's a tremble to her tone that makes me hate myself for causing it.

"Us." I stand there, before her, hope gone. "There's only one way for this to end and it's badly.

One step.

Two more.

She stops, afraid to come closer.

Afraid of me?

She swallows hard enough for me to hear. "It doesn't have to."

"But it will. Are you ready to take the fall? Cuz there's no going up, sweetheart. It's downhill from here."

"We can keep things light. Fun—"

"And games."

"I wasn't going to say that."

"You didn't have to. What do you want from me?"

"I want your friendship. I want your—"

"And what?" I ask, leaning on the counter and crossing my arms over my chest. My feelings may be hurt, but I'm in no hurry to leave them bleeding at her feet in the Financial District. "Just say it. Friendship and what?"

"Support."

Friend-zoned. Just like that I've been taken out of the running. "And there it is." A smirk comes out, but it's more one of disbelief than anything else. "Let me ask you something. How'd you get Lowry to come to The Hideaway that night? For real."

She shifts on her feet, the red dress loose in the front from hanging open in the back. "I talked one of the receptionists he's always hitting on into going out. She suggested The Hideaway. Katie had been trying to get me to go there for months. So I casually on purpose made sure Lowry knew we'd be there that night and he told me to text him the address."

"You walked in alone. What happened to the other woman?"

"Her married boyfriend called. When he calls that means he's free from his wife and kids, so she has to be ready to meet him on a moment's notice." The image of my boss's ex-wife crying in Saks Fifth Avenue instantly comes to mind. She continues, "I didn't bother to text Lowry that she had cancelled."

"He was possessive of you."

"He feels very protective of the women in the office even if he has no interest in us."

"When you left with him, did he think you were going home with him?"

"Yes." She comes closer and leans her hip against the counter next to me. "He touched me on the leg in the car and tried to kiss me."

"That's what you wanted."

"I don't want it in the back of a car where he gets off then gets out and leaves me riding home alone."

"What do you expect from him? What do you want?"

"I want love, Hardy."

"You're looking in the wrong place then, sweetheart. I know that asshole. I used to be that asshole. So when I say we are going to end badly—you and I, you and this Lowry dude are going to be disastrous."

"Don't say that."

"I'm not going to lie to you anymore. I can't protect you from self-destructing, but I will tell you what I'm going to do for you."

"What is that?"

"I'm going to stay. I'm going to give you the friendship and support you want from me."

"Why?"

"Because when he fucks you on New Year's and then he's flirting with the receptionist the next day, you're going to need a friend." I take her hand and hold it between us. "I'll be that friend for you."

Tears fill her eyes and she falls into my arms. I wrap them around her and kiss the top of her head. The pain I feel now won't compare to the pain I know she's going to experience with that asshole. Like how I knew she needed to feel bad for hurting me, she needs to go through with her plan so she will eventually see she had me all along.

Chapter Seventeen

Virginia and I have come to an understanding. Or should I say, I've come to my senses. No more visits to the hipster. I was right all along. Love blinds you to reality. I've taken off my rose-colored glasses. I might have actually stomped them into smithereens before I climbed into bed with her.

Before you say, "But Hardy, she shot you down," let me explain. When I decided to stay and support our friendship, I meant it. Maybe it's the ridiculous notion of it's better to have whatever I can versus nothing at all if I'd walked out that door. Or maybe despite the bullshit I spew, an inkling, or better yet, smaller than an inkling whatever that is, of hope still exists. A lot like that seed that was planted when I met her it's there still, rolling around in the dirt that is self-respect. I can feel it like the princess felt the pea, but since it's me, it's more like the king and his . . . whatever. You get the drift.

So here I am, lying next to her, watching a romantic comedy that I don't think is funny at all. That might be because Virginia's and my relationship resembles the mess

I'm watching a little too closely. "Ultimately, she's still cheating," I say, pointing at the screen like Meg Ryan will stop her nonsense and break up with her boyfriend before pursuing Tom Hanks. "Oh, her last name is Ryan, like you."

"We're not related."

"Too bad."

"I know. I could use a vacation to LA about now." She lifts her head, and asks, "Are you hungry?"

"I can eat."

Using my chest as leverage, she lifts up and shoots an eyebrow up in amusement. "You did earlier—twice. Once at Kate & Theo and then me."

"Did you set me up for that lame joke?"

"No." She laughs. "I'm actually hungry. The food was good but the portions were tiny. Want to go out and get something to eat?"

"You do realize it's almost midnight, right?"

"Come on. Where's your sense of adventure, Hardy?"

"Back in Brooklyn where I know I can get a great sandwich in the middle of the night at the local deli."

"Well I can beat it."

"Wanna bet?"

"I'll bet you the food."

"You're on." We flip our feet to the floor and start pulling on our clothes and shoes again. I peek over at her on the other side of the bed. She was lounging in sweatpants and a The Resistance T-shirt she got from their tour a few months back. I flicked the pic of the lead singer that covers the front when she talked about how hot he was live and she felt like he was singing just for her. I rolled my eyes and flicked her again before realizing I had actually flicked her nipple. After she said, "Ouch," and rubbed it, she admitted it felt pretty good.

That was a happy side effect that I'd love to explore more with her sometime, but since our earlier talk, I need to back off. I also need to be careful or she'll have me face over fist in deep shit feels for her all over again. So naturally I immediately accepted her invitation to watch the movie with her in bed. That's where she has her DVD player plugged in. I didn't even know they still made DVD players. Don't we just download movies these days?

Guess not.

She pauses the movie and stands up. "You ready?"

"As I'll ever be. Where are you taking me?"

"That's for me to know and you to find out."

She's so happy that I don't want to burst her bubble by telling her I really should be going home. I don't want to burst my happy bubble either. That seed is sprouting from hope to fate, and I believe wholeheartedly in destiny. It's what I've used to guide my own life. Maybe I need to trust in it when it comes to my love life.

The doorman is surprised to see use when we exit the building. As if we're a couple, Virginia's arm slides around mine and our fingers weave together and we hold hands. "Your hands are fucking freezing," I say, surprised her hands feel colder than a witch's tit.

"Sorry," she says like she's not really that sorry. "You're so warm. God, I need your hands warming my body."

Big Richard stirs. "Please don't say things like that. We may have gotten off but I haven't had sex since I met you and words like *warm* and *hands on your body* kind of remind my dick that he's not slipped into a woman's sleeping bag in a while."

"Ewwww. A woman's sleeping bag? Gross."

"I was trying to be polite. Would you rather me say pussy? Because I have no problem saying pussy."

"Apparently, and you just did twice. Also, you sure didn't mind saying it earlier."

"Earlier I was eating your pussy. We were in the moment. Now we're walking down the street, to who knows where in the world, holding hands."

"Was that you romancing me, Hardy?"

"Nope. But if I was, would it be working?"

"Totally." She leans her head on my shoulder, and squeezes my hand tighter. "Sleeping bags are cozy and comfy and warm, like sweatpants. And you know I like those."

"See, I'm playing to my audience."

"You're generous like that, and you're warming my hands up."

Warming cold hands. Gloves are great for that. "Oh, I almost forgot." I reach inside my coat pocket and pull out the gloves. "I got you these."

Her feet come to a sudden halt and she takes the gloves from me. "You bought me gloves?"

"Yeah, earlier tonight."

"You bought me gloves earlier tonight from Bendel's?"

"I did." I reach over and touch them again. "They're cashmere."

"Hardy, I don't know what to say."

"You don't have to say anything. Just wear them."

She pulls them off the hanger and slides her hands into them. "Oh my God. These are heaven. Heaven, I tell you." Her body is clinging to mine, her arms wrapped around my neck cutting off my airway. "This is one of the most thoughtful gifts I've ever received."

I loosen the noose of her arms, and cough. "They're only gloves, V.""You don't understand. I was shopping today and every store was sold out. I was so disappointed, but here you are taking me to dinner at an impossible to get a reservation restaurant and pulling gloves from your pocket like they magically appeared after a wish. I don't know where you came from, Hardy Richard, but I'm so fortunate to have you in my life. Thank you for the gloves. I love them."

"You're very welcome."

She kisses my cheek and then takes my hand again. This time her hand is fuzzy and warm. Similar to my feelings right now.

Excitedly, she points, and announces, "There."

"A hotdog stand?" I'm not disappointed but I am surprised. "I wasn't filling enough?"

I'm elbowed. "You were too filling. As for food, let's eat."

Five minutes later, I'm standing on the corner of a Manhattan street holding the cart owner's last two dogs while she carefully pulls the gloves off her hands and tucks them in her pockets.

Two minutes after that, she's tossed the napkins and devoured the hot dog and she's putting the gloves on like they are gold rings. I almost expect her to call them her precious. Freaky bastard.

We walk faster this time, both of us cold. Before we reach the building, she asks, "Will you stay?"

No build up or word foreplay. She just throws it out there like the opening pitch at the start of baseball season, and I catch it. *Yes. Yes. Yes.* "Sure," I reply casually with a shrug, pretending I could take the offer or leave it.

What? Did you expect me to say no because of earlier? I'm a guy. We get over shit quick. Feelings are handled by hiding or ignoring them completely. If an emotion decides to hang around too long it basically becomes a round of hide the sausage. You know, tuck it here. Tuck it there. Tuck it anywhere you can shove it. Preferably into a warm, wet— the door to her building is opened.

The doorman is onto us. I'm sure he has a second sense for couples getting it on. He's looking me over like an over-protective older brother, which thank God, she doesn't have. Brothers can be real dicks to deal with when it comes to dating their sisters. Especially if said sister, after she begs you to hide said earlier sausage inside her, has an overly steroided brother bust into her room and start a fight while yelling, "Mine" and "Hands off my girl." And the classic, "I will kill you."

Then, as you're running out the door with your frank n' beans covered, you see them making up with a kiss. Yeah, now that's a horrifying sight that stays with you long after you find out they're stepsiblings, and they just met two years earlier. They're still fucking. Christmas at their house must be very entertaining.

I've just heard of this kind of thing happening. It's never happened to me. Nope . . . Not to me. But I digress . . .

I nod as we pass by and go back upstairs. In the elevator, we're quiet. It's late. We're tired, and probably have too much on our minds. Things have really changed the last couple of weeks, and I never saw it coming. Even my initial blindside has been blindsided. I sneak a glimpse of her just as she's sneaking one of me. What must she think of me? What goes on inside that pretty head of hers? I sometimes wonder if she feels the same about me as I do her. Communicating those feelings could probably set things straight, but what's the fun in that? Aren't our twenties about fumbling around trying to find ourselves, and hoping love finds us along the way? Fuck, who knows? I sure don't. Anyway, she's made her choice more than clear.

Lowry on New Year's Eve. The plan is already in

motion in her head. The asshole wins. He gets the girl, her midnight kiss, and being seduced at the Waldorf-Astoria.

Check. Check. And double check. Game. Set. Match.

Fuck my love life.

I was doing just fine before that four-letter word wasn't around cock-blocking me to the pretties at the bar, and over-complicating my life in general. If she wants him, she can have him. As for me, it's all systems go and moving forward with the plan in place. Its not like I have any right to gripe about her sleeping with someone else. She's single, and we're not a couple.

Fuck. I can't even believe I let the C-word slip from my mouth. Like the hipster warned, I need to watch my language.

When we enter the apartment, I help her with her coat and hang it on the hook. She takes her gloves off, and says, "Thank you again for these."

"You're welcome." Silence starts to extend the distance that stands between us as I take my coat off and hang it up.

"Glass of water?" she asks from the kitchen.

"Sure."

She comes back into the living room and hands me a tall glass. "Thank you for staying. I know . . . well, just know I want you here, Hardy."

For some reason, my damn heart refuses to leave my sleeve. "I want to be here with you."

Taking my hand, we walk into the bedroom together. She goes to the left side of the bed and sets her water on the nightstand, so I walk to the right side, setting mine down. "Guess you sleep on the left. Good thing because I sleep on the right."

"It's like we're made for each other." With that left

behind lingering in the air around me, she goes into the bathroom and shuts the door.

I think I stare at that door for a good three minutes, maybe longer, her words replaying through my head. By the time I settle on the fact that she might have just admitted that she's actually attracted to me I've already hashtagged that sucker and pocketed it for later in my notes app. Seems maybe my feelings aren't as unwarranted as I once thought. Maybe. Just maybe *we are made for each other*.

#MFEO

Chapter Eighteen

I stand there like a goof, not sure what I'm supposed to be doing, so I undress like I was earlier, down to my boxer briefs and socks because my feet are cold. We change places—she crawls under the covers in her sweatpants and Resistance T-shirt and I go to the bathroom. Before the door closes, she says, "I set out a toothbrush for you."

"Thanks."

The blue brush is fully loaded with striped paste, so I wet it and go to town. I can only imagine how my breath is after shoving a wiener down my throat. *Wait, what?* Hot dog. Dirty birds.

While I scrub my pearly whites, I do what any guest would do—dig through the medicine cabinet and the one under the sink. There's nothing too interesting other than *everything*. It's like a mecca for nosy people who like to go the extra mile and snoop through people's stuff. Cough drops, Vick's VapoRub, Advil, Emergen-C packets, toothbrush and paste, an out of date prescription for Amoxicillin, tampons, and what do we have here—a box of extra large condoms in ribbed for her pleasure vanilla flavored. Damn, that's got a lot going on. Whatever happened to it being used for protection? I like that she's prepared. I now must torture-tease her about it.

I spit, rinse, and wrap up my business before taking the black box with neon yellow writing to bed with me. The overhead light is off and the room is dim except for the lamp on her nightstand. I climb under the fluffy blanket and toss the box on the bed between us.

Virginia's gaze lands on it and her eyebrows shoot up. So to push this a bit further than I should for entertainment purposes only, I ask, "Do you have a vibrator?"

"Hardy," she cautions, warning, or more like wanting, to end this already.

"Do you?"

She grabs her pillow and drags it flat down and flops back, then pulls the awesomely soft blanket over her head. "Yes."

"Show me."

The blanket is flapped down with authority. "No."

"Yes." I move down and rest on my elbow.

"No." The firmness of her tone seconds earlier is teetering on giving in.

Reaching over, I rub my hand over her stomach. And even though I'm damn jealous that rock band gets to hang out on her chest, I get the pleasure of sliding it up and getting the real thing. I lean down and kiss her stomach while dipping my fingertips under the waistband of her sweatpants. "I want to watch you pleasure yourself."

The scoff comes out stuck in the middle of a belly laugh. "No way."

"Why? Do you know how hot that is?" I lie back and close my eyes. "Thinking about you touching yourself like that, getting off." I grab more than a handful of my dick. "It turns me on just thinking about it."

Her voice is lower, the hint of debate heard. "I can't, Hardy."

Turning to look at her, I keep stroking my cock. "You can. Remember, with us, there is no judgment. No negativity. Just us. Just pleasure." I lean over and kiss the side of her mouth while rubbing her hip. Pressing my erection against her leg, a slow gyrate begins. "You smell so good, and feel even better. Do you know how much you turn me on?"

An exhale of breath is heard from her nose before she gives in and opens her mouth for more air. "I can feel you, but when I do, I want you more than lesson three."

I roll to my back. Putting my arms over my eyes, I release my own hard breath. "God. Me too. So much."

"Maybe we—"

I look at her. "No."

"Why?"

"Because the first time should matter and if we have sex right now it won't be about you, but me."

"I don't care." Now she moves to her side and rubs over my stomach and begins going lower. "I want to be with you."

Grabbing her wrist, I stop her hand from reaching its intended destination. "I want to be with you so much. This is not just hard for me, it's almost impossible, but I won't treat you like every other guy out there. This is important to me. You've respected yourself enough to hold off. I'm just asking you to hold on a little longer."

She lies back and as much as I hate that her hands aren't on me, it's not the right time, but I know when is. "What are you doing next Saturday?"

A slow smiles slides into place, just how I like her—happy. "That's my birthday."

"I know."

When her eyes meet mine, she asks, "I was hoping to spend it with you. I didn't know if you'd be able to get off work two Saturdays in a row."

Hoarding in on her real estate, I make myself more comfortable and rest my head on her pillow. "Have you forgotten I'm the boss?"

"It's hard to forget how bossy you are when you're always reminding me," she teases.

I pull her close and wrap my arm around her and spank her playfully on that fine ass of hers, then get a solid grab. Because I can.

She snuggles against me and closes her eyes. Then I whisper, "Can I take you out for your birthday, V?"

Her body is relaxed and molded to mine. You know those feelings I've been walking around with on my sleeve that I can't seem to shake? Yeah, they crawl up into my chest making the beats bounce around my ribcage wildly. Holding her is just what I needed. She's not just warming my arms. She's setting my soul on fire.

"I'd love that. Thank you."

I stroke her hair and kiss her head. "Thank you, sweet girl." Closing my eyes, I whisper, "Sweet dreams."

"Sweet dreams."

The woman needs blackout curtains. This blinding light is ridiculous. "Fuck," I groan, rolling away from the window. "Who the fuck is shining a spotlight in here?"

Her laugh is light and the bed shakes a little. She leans her forehead against mine and says, "That's called the sun. I know you work nights, but this is what morning looks like."

Grabbing a pillow, I cover my head. "Morning is overrated. Let's go back to sleep until a more sociable time. I'm partial to two."

She slinks under the pillow and kisses my nose. "I can't sleep anymore. I'm going to make coffee. Can I bring you a cup?"

"What time is it?"

"Seven thirty."

"Yes, I'd like a cup . . . in about five hours."

Laughing again, the bed moves when she starts to leave. I grab her wrist, and then her leg, and drag her back under the covers. "Stay."

Without protest, she shifts and wraps her arms around me. I rest my head on her chest, letting the steady beat of her heart lull me back to sleep.

The next time I open my eyes, I'm alone in bed.

Which is wrong on so many levels.

I hear Christmas music playing softly in the other room. I flip the covers off and pad across the floor ignoring the massive boner I'm sporting. He can be handled in a moment. I peek into the living room and see Virginia sitting on the floor with wrapping paper and presents all around her.

Visions of a fast forward future: fire burning in a fireplace, music playing, her sitting surrounded by toys and a plate of cookies and milk comes to mind, completely freaking me out.

Boner. Gone. Just like that.

I duck back and get dressed. After a quick visit to the bathroom, I come out to find her standing in the doorway with a pink cup of coffee outstretched. "Good morning. I thought you might like this."

"A travel mug?"

"Coffee to go. I figured you'd be ready to bolt when you

got up," she says with a smile that would devastate me if I weren't already freaked out from the future that flashed before my eyes.

"Yeah." I shift under her analyzing gaze.

I take the pink cup. "I'm supposed to open the bar."

"It's okay, Hardy. We don't have to make this awkward." Standing there looking at me like I'm a problem she's trying to solve—the numbers out of whack and making no sense until she finds the missing factor, she adds, "I never expected you to stay."

Well that made it awkward. Moving closer, I touch her cheek, hating that I don't just hear the disappointment in her voice, but I see it in her eyes. "I'll see you Saturday." She nods, her words not coming when she moves closer and rests her cheek against my chest. I hug her. Tight. For her. For me. "Saturday, okay?"

"Okay."

"Look at me," I say, leaning back. When she does, I smile. "I'm glad I stayed."

Her smile grows and she tightens her hold around my middle. "Me too." Lifting up, she kisses my lips gently and instead of dropping down, she stays. I close my eyes and savor the taste of her sweet lips. Then I kiss her back.

There's no tongue and our hands stay above the waist, which is hard because she's wearing these little shorts that hug her hips and barely cover that ass of hers. Why she wasn't wearing these last night in bed, I have no idea, but the sweatpants are getting burned next time I stay over.

I weave my fingers into her hair and hold her there, realizing I wish I didn't have to go. Her lips are soft and caressing. This just might be my favorite kiss of all time—easy, uncomplicated, simple. So good that I start to think maybe we don't have to end badly after all. Maybe we don't have to end at all.

She steps back, our hands still clasped. That look that's starting to become a regular fixture in the green of her eyes is there, the corners at the top rounded and the bottom in a point. I don't say anything because I'm not so sure that my brown eyes are doing the same.

Walking me to the door, she says, "I'll see you next Saturday."

"I'll text you."

The door is opened and she leans against it watching me walk through. I turn and catch her eyes on my ass. I wink, and say, "My eyes are up here, sweetheart."

Just as cocky, she raises an eyebrow at me. "My eyes are up here but that didn't stop you from getting a parting eyeful of my tits."

Shrugging, I laugh. "Can't wait to see those perky girls again."

"Maybe you'll get lucky next weekend. We still have one lesson left."

Walking backward to the elevator, I let my gaze graze over her toned legs. I look up and smile while raising my arms out wide. "I'm a sure thing, honey, so you're definitely getting lucky next weekend." I punch the elevator button.

When the elevator arrives, I wave and say, "See you, Virginia."

"See you, Hardy."

I step on and am smiling like a loon. The lady already on the elevator pulls her little daughter under her arm and covers her ears. I can't stop from laughing, but I give them their space. I'm tempted to spew a slew of curses just to make the hand-muffs worth the effort, but I behave.

When we get to the lobby, she scurries off, but the little girl says, "Goodbye."

Smiling, I reply "Goodbye."

They leave quickly. The doorman continues holding the door for me. "Good morning."

"Good morning."

Just as I step outside, he adds, "Ms. Ryan sure is a lovely woman."

"She sure is." I smile and look back, thinking he has more on his mind than just a nice comment about V.

"She never has guests over." I nod, wondering where this is going. He continues, "It's good to see she had company."

Standing under the awning, I look at him, digesting the information he's sharing. *She never has any company?* I smile too big to let him in on why. I'll just look like an asshole. I'll leave that role to the asshole himself at her work, but I can't not say something, so I do, "You'll be seeing a lot more of me." *Claim. Staked.*

He nods, his own smile in place. "Good to hear."

I shake the doorman's hand. "I'm Hardy Richard, by the way."

"Barry Rusk."

"Good to meet you, Barry."

"You too. Have a good day, Mr. Richard."

"Thank you. I plan on having a great day." He tips his cap to me and I tip my imaginary one to him.

Great indeed. With three lessons down and one left that I've been saving for her birthday, the best is yet to come.

Do I really have to say it?

Fine. *You win.*

The best is yet to come. *Literally and figuratively.*

Chapter Nineteen

I don't want to teach her.

I want to win her.

I want to be with her.

I don't know when this change came over me. I can think of a million little things that swayed me to take notice of Virginia Ryan: utterly endearing smile, that little inch long scar on the side of her right kneecap, the way she smells of vanilla, or even the way her lips fall open when she falls apart from touching her in that most heavenly of places.

But I know the truth. Deep down I know.

The minute my Paloma walked into the bar, she walked right into my heart and claimed it as her own. It's been two days since I left her apartment and I don't think I've gone five minutes without thinking about her. I've been working long shifts, on purpose. Working beats sitting around beating off on my own. Well, I've done that too. I mean, I have fresh memories to get off to. I can almost taste V on my tongue if I close my eyes and remember her legs spread before me, her head pressed to the window for all to see us. Fuck, I'm hard again.

I tuck the bar rag into the front of my pants and tell Leo, the newest person, who's a bartender and model, to join the team, "I've got to make a call . . . in the back."

"Is that what the kids are calling it? A phone call?"

"Hey, you haven't been here long enough to give me a hard time."

"Doesn't seem like I'm the one giving you a hard time, and if I am, then we need to have a talk."

"Fuck you," I say, flipping him off while shaking my head. I turn to leave. Fucker is funny. And ballsy. The ladies are going to love him.

I'm gone just over an hour. I went home to have lunch and deal with this situation in my pants. It took two spurt sessions to get out the pent up desire I have for that woman. Feeling relieved and less irritated, I leave my apartment and grab a ham and Swiss on the way back to the bar. I'm fucking starving.

When I round the corner to the street of The Hideaway, I stop and duck into a coffee shop's doorway. Peeking around and staring, I'm not even sure why I'm hiding.

"Hardy?"

My face is plastered to the window when I jump from the sound of my name behind me. "Fuck."

Laughter tinkles behind me. A hand takes my arm. "Sorry," she says, "I didn't mean to scare you."

"Hey Luisa." I shrug and tug at the bottom of my coat to straighten it. "No, no, you didn't."

"You sure about that? By looking at the face print you left smeared on my window, I think you might be kidding yourself there, buddy."

"I never kid myself." Virginia comes to mind immediately. "Okay, maybe sometimes."

"Anyway, who are we hiding from?"

"Not hiding. I don't even know why I ducked under. It's my parents."

"Ohhhh," she replies, looking around the corner. "Do you not get along with them?"

"No, I actually get along with them great." I catch a glimpse down the sidewalk. They've gone inside. "I think I'm just not in the mood to be interrogated about my life, and when I say life, I mean love life."

Laughing, she wipes down one of the bistro tables. "I see. So how is the love life? Has anyone managed to catch the eye of the unhookable Hardy Richard?"

"Ha! Good one."

"Even funnier because it's true."

"Maybe."

She squeals and jumps up. "Maybe funnier because it's true or maybe because someone caught your eye?"

"Aren't they sort of the same thing?"

"Maybe." She laughs again. "So tell me."

Walking back onto the sidewalk, I smile and raise an eyebrow. "Let's just say . . . maybe." I leave her with that, now laughing myself.

"You're incorrigible, Hardy."

"So I'm told."

I reach the bar and pull the door wide open. Time to face the music. My eyes haven't even adjusted between the glaring white of the snow outside and the dim lighting inside when I hear that familiar clasping of hands, and then, "Hardy, darling."

"Hi Mom. Hi Dad."

Leo stands up from behind the bar with a bottle of champagne in hand. "Your parents are here."

"Yeah, thanks for the heads up."

"My pleasure. Or maybe it's been yours for the last two hours."

Glaring, I remind, "My parents are here."

"I know," he replies, chuckling. Leo's busy pouring three glasses while I hug my mom and then my dad because he's become a huggy bastard since he retired.

"What brings you by?" I hand them each a glass.

My mom tilts hers to tap against mine. "Cheers."

After we drink, my dad leads us to a table. "We were in the neighborhood."

We settle in, and I ask, "Brooklyn? That's quite a ways from the neighborhood of another state."

"Connecticut's not that far," my mom says. "Anyway, we wanted to get some shopping done in the city." She looks around. "The place is looking good. You're keeping it very clean."

"We have a service. They're paid well."

"Good. No one wants to hang out in a sticky, stanky bar. A nice kempt establishment brings in nice kempt customers."

"Yes, we like catering to our upscale clientele."

My dad says, "So business is good?"

"Solid. I might need to hire a few more bartenders in the new year. I'm also considering bringing on some wait staff." I take a sip and set the glass down and spin it by the stem between my fingers. "Remember Eddie? I just gave him a promotion to help manage the place. I'm going to start focusing more on the overall operations."

My mom smiles. "You hoped when you left New York

finance you would not work as much, but here you are working more I suspect."

"This time it's for me—solely and good for my soul."

She asks, "Speaking of souls, you mentioned at the fundraiser that you might have met someone? How is that going?"

"If I remember correctly, I told you I didn't."

"Do you really think I don't know your tells. I've known them since you were three, Hardy. You couldn't hide behind a lie then and you can't now, so tell us so we don't have to worry about you."

"You don't have to worry about me. I'm good."

"Happy?"

"I'm happy." Medium. Her lips purse. "Fine. Mostly."

"Who is she?" Dad asks. Leo makes a round, topping off our glasses.

"It's complicated. I don't want you getting invested when we're not meant to be."

"We care about you and if you care about her, then we're invested already," my mom says.

"That's so pressuring, Mom. Don't you see?"

My dad leans his elbows on the table. "You know what I see, Son?"

Sitting back, I cross my arms over my chest. I can tell this isn't going to be as quick as I thought. "What?"

He says, "You and your sister have been so busy with your careers that neither of you have even a second in your day to spare for the stuff that matters at the end of it."

"I—"

His hands go up. "No, Hardy. I want you to listen to your mother and me."

I drop my reactions and relax, willing to hear them out.

He continues, "I worked hard for thirty-five years and what did that get me?"

"A five bedroom colonial in New Canaan and a retirement that you and Mom can actually survive off and live nicely."

"Yes, it did, but it's this woman next to me," he says, taking my mom's hand, "that really made it all worth it. She gave me purpose."

"I have purpose, Dad. I like my life."

My mom leans in. "What your father is trying to tell you is we want to sell the house and travel the world at our leisure without the heavy ties of a mortgage. Do you understand what that means?"

"No."

"It means we can't do that because our children are unsettled in their lives."

"Sabrina and I are fine. She's got an amazing job overseas and I have the bar and my life here. Don't let us hold you back from doing what you want to do."

"You're not understanding. If something happens to us, we don't want you to be alone. I've read about The Hideaway. You have wonderful reviews, but there's mention, more than once, of a . . ." She lowers her voice to a mouse's whisper, "Sexual undercurrent."

"Oh God, please don't ever say anything like that again. Gross."

"Stop being ridiculous. We're all adults here. Sex is a natural part of living a full life."

"*Mommm.* No. Stop." She laughs and I think I catch my dad sliding his hand up and down her thigh. Ew. I stand. "Look. I'm going to be very frank with you. There is a girl, a woman actually, that I am interested in. She's beautiful, and tastes like vanilla ice cream on a hot August day. She carries the color of the changing leaves at the end of summer in her eyes. And without a doubt, what I want to do to her perfect mouth is probably illegal in most states." The sins she makes me want to commit make my dick ache.

"Virginia's beauty is more than skin deep." Deep. God, I want to fuck her so bad. "She's kind and thoughtful. Spirited, and when she looks at me, she sees the person I want to be, the person she believes I can be, and damn do I want to be that guy for her."

I didn't plan on breaking out into some lovesick soliloquy, but here I am, standing in an empty bar pouring out all those cramped emotions I've been pocketing onto a table in front of my parents and Leo. When I look up, Clive and Eddie are standing near the back door with boxes of scotch in their arms. Leo starts a slow clap and soon the scotch is set down and I'm getting the worst of golf clap ovations. When my parents stand and join in, the applause builds.

Flipping everyone off, I laugh. "I really hate you guys." I don't and they know it, but I hate this shiny happy shit. Kind of. Sort of. Only when I'm at the center of it.

My mom comes around the table, and says, "Bring Virginia over for dinner sometime. We'd love to meet her."

My dad claps me on the back, and says, "Or better yet, kiss her and seal that deal on New Year's. You know what they say about that holiday. Whatever you're doing at midnight on New Year's Eve, is what you'll be doing all year long."

If that's the case, I can think of a million other things other than kissing I'd like to be doing with her at midnight. Or to her. Or in her. Or her to me. Or together. I think that's what he means. Be together. #MFEO and all that junk.

I follow my parents as they head for the door. I'm thinking they've had enough of our antics to hold them over for quite some time. "Thanks for coming to see me. I actually feel better, more determined to make this thing with Virginia less complicated and more simple."

"When it's right, it's easy." She hugs me at the door. "I've never seen you with that look of love in your eyes before. It looks good on you."

I'm not one for blushing, but the embarrassment I feel makes my face feel hot. "Thanks, Mom."

"You're welcome. Now go get the girl." Her hands go up in a silent cheer just like she did when I was ten and won the regional spelling bee. I might be shaking my head, but my mom is the best.

My dad adds, "And try kissing first. That tends to win a lady's heart. Save the illegal stuff for the bedroom." He gives me that buddy-buddy wink. "But if you do get yourself in a spot of trouble, call me and I'll bail you out."

"You know I didn't really mean I would do something to her that would get me arrested, right?" Unless she wants me to, and then who am I to deny her needs and wants. But to be on the safe side, I should probably look into where "fucking one's mouth" falls legally in the state of New York. If it is illegal, it wouldn't be the first time I've committed the crime with her, but it's hard to say no when—What the fuck tangent have I gone off on?

After saying goodbye to them, I turn and see the guys still standing around watching me turn into a full on unstoppable train wreck. "Get back to work and never, I mean never, mention any of this again."

Clive is too busy laughing. Leo is suddenly super busy scrubbing a spot on the bar top, but I see that damn mocking grin. Eddie salutes me, and says, "You got it, boss." He sets his box on a table, and adds, "But just so you know, the guys and I have discussed the matter and we approve."

"Approve of what?"

"Virginia. She meets all the magical unicorn criteria: sexy as all get out, intelligent, and she's really nice."

I want to hide from the teasing I've endured, but he's right. She is sexy and smart, but it's that last part that matters most. "She is nice."

"Really," starts Clive, "she's too good for you, so if she's giving you a shot, you should take it."

"Fuck you very much, Clive."

"No problem. We're here to keep your ego in check."

"You're doing a solid job."

"That's why we're paid the big bucks," Eddie jokes.

"You're paid the big bucks for your pretty boy faces that bring in the pretty bills."

We laugh. It's good to joke with the guys. We're more than co-workers. We're friends. I can count on any of them if I was ever in a bind, and they know they can count on me. Walking in from the back, Romeo tugs his beanie off and asks, "What'd I miss?" "Our fearless leader is in love," Leo asserts.

Romeo nods, another annoying grin is on his face as if he stole the other fella's. "It was only a matter of time before he realized it. Now that you have, Hardy, time to lock that girl down. And if you don't, I'm sure one of us will be more than happy to."

"She'd never go for one of you jackoffs. Like Eddie said, she's smart." I head for the office. "The show's over. My life is back off limits. Get to work and let's kick tonight's ass."

Chapter Twenty

My dick has become hard like a dead log in winter. I just hope it won't break. By the pain in my pants, I'm not so sure it won't. I haven't gone this long without having actual sex since I was in high school. Fine, college. I like to aggrandize my memories from back then. Like Virginia, I went through an awkward stage. Okay, not as awkward as her, but now I look at her photo from high school and I see the beautiful woman she's turned into. I don't even have to stretch the imagination. That much. She's there under those braces, glasses, and stringy hair. If I had known her then, I would have hit on her.

Seriously, I would have. She's the same person.

I don't want to pummel V our first time together. Finding balance means one too many hand jobs in the meantime. We've barely texted, both of us more busy with work than we'd like as the year starts coming to a close. She's been working late most nights and I'm working every night this week so I can get Saturday off. It's been a good distraction.

You know what's not?

Isabella Collins.

And here I thought it would be just another Thursday night. I sense her the second she and the storm that swarms around her enter The Hideaway. Checking my watch. 9:37 p.m. There's something about her being here at this hour on a school night that tells me trouble just walked in.

Her eyes are on me the moment she walks in, which sucks because she catches my eyes on her. I look down quickly, pretending to wash glasses. She knows me better than I'd like to admit, though to *my* credit, she only really knows the old me—asshole investment advisor, modern loft with massive parties, and two thousand dollar suits. Well the suits haven't changed. I still like a nice suit and my watch collection, but I don't have to wear them every day. Only when I want. Wonder if I should wear my charcoal Vittori on our date. Date is used loosely since Virginia friend-zoned me last weekend. After Saturday, I'm going to be dancing in her end zone though.

"Hello, Hardy."

Looking up, I see Isabella. I'd almost forgotten about her. *Almost.* "Slumming, Isabella?"

"You're always raving about Brooklyn, so I thought I'd come visit."

I rest my palms on the bar, and ask, "Are you visiting the borough or me?"

"Can't I be doing both?"

"You were always one for ulterior motives."

She slips onto the stool in front of me. "You know what I like."

I do. She's predictable in every way. In other words, she's the complete opposite of Virginia. While making her vodka soda, I start trying to remember what attracted me to Isabella in the first place. It's been a while since I've thought back to those days in detail. Mostly because so much of it was blurred by the booze. It's funny that now that I own a bar, I drink less overall. Most days I don't drink at all. Tonight, thanks to the woman sitting in front of me, won't be one of those days. I twist the lime into the drink and add a lime peel curly on the top. I still have standards, even if I despise the customer.I grab a glass and pour a whiskey neat for myself. I take a good pull before setting it down, and asking, "What really brings you by?"

"You."

"I was afraid of that."

"Nothing to be afraid of. I've just been thinking about you."

The bar is fairly calm at this time, so Clive has it handled. When I turn back to her, I say, "Don't. Don't think about me. You're married. We've been long over."

Her index finger runs the rim of her glass several times. "What if we didn't have to be?"

"I don't date married women." I give the most obvious out to end this.

"What if I wasn't married anymore?"

I take another long drink of the alcohol before I burst out laughing. The insult is seen in her eyes since most of her face doesn't move. "I wish I could say I was surprised."

"Maybe some sympathy is in order."

"What game are you trying to play? We did nothing but fight."

"We were young."

"We're not that much older. Four years."

"I feel like I've lived a lifetime in that four years." She takes a sip and then says, "I caught him fucking his secretary." This time the glass is to her lips much longer and when the glass is set down, half is gone.

"I'm sorry." I mean it too. No one deserves to be cheated on and in such a cliché manner makes it worse. "Are you still together?"

"No. I left a month ago. He's fighting me on all fronts—financially and for custody of our son. I haven't gotten to see him in three weeks."

My head is shaking in disgust before she finishes. We may not have been #MFEO but kids need both parents, even if separately. I cover her hand because I'm not heartless. I can tell she needs a friend or a bartender. This comes with the territory. "You deserve better and I have no doubt the final judgment will be in your favor."

Her hand covers mine. "Thank you. I knew you'd understand."

"Hi."

Just right of her, the brunette I've been dying to see all week is standing with a grimace on her face, her eyes on my hand that's currently comforting Isabella. I slide it out and wipe it on my pants. "Hey, V, you're here?" It comes out like a question though I didn't intend it that way.

"My apologies. Did I interrupt?" Virginia looks at Isabella before her gaze returns to me.

I'm about to speak, but Isabella beats me to it, "Yes."

"No," I correct. "No, you didn't." I hurry from behind the bar and come around to the front. Taking Virginia's glove covered hand, I nod toward the back. "Want to talk in private?"

I start to walk, but her feet stay firmly planted to the spot. "Do we need to talk in private, Hardy?"

"What? No, I was only offering since you just got here." I'm babbling like a guilty fucking fool. *Shit.* I need to fix this. "It's good to see you." I lean forward to kiss her on the cheek but she backs out of reach. *Shit. Shit. Shit.*

She sits down on the stool next to Isabella and I don't like the looks of this at all. Until I remember that we are friends. Only friends, according to her. And since she's all about the asshole still, I don't owe her anything. Nothing but a drink, and a fuck on Saturday, but that's beside the current point I'm trying to make. I start to make a Paloma and dump ice in the tall glass, but she says, "I'll have what she's having."

Shit. She's mad.

Fortunately they use the same glass. I start pouring vodka that I personally like and give her a little extra. It's not like she's driving home or anything. While I'm cocktail concocting, Isabella turns to Virginia, who's taking her coat and gloves off, and says, "Hello. I'm Isabella Treaton of Connecticut."

Maiden name. She used her maiden name. I think the trouble I mentioned walking in before has just become a quicksand trap. I'm not falling for it.

"We've met before. When I was out with Hardy at a restaurant in the city. I'm Virginia Ryan of Manhattan."

How she says that with a straight face is beyond me but I'm going to give her extra special sexual love on Saturday for doing it. Isabella's gaze head to toes her, and then says, "Manhattan. Huh? I would have surely thought one of the outer boroughs."

Oh shit.

Just when Virginia is about to roar, I say, "Did you know that hippos are too dense to really be buoyant to swim so they are considered semi-aquatic animals who jog or run up to fifteen miles an hour under water?"

Both women are staring at me, and my mind goes blank under the harsh glares. Virginia finally says, "Lowry asked me if I would be at the holiday party."

I grab my glass and down the rest of the whiskey. When I slam it down on the bar mat, I shake my head. I thought I was at a loss for words before, but now I have plenty I'd like to say, but seeing as this is my establishment, it would be unprofessional to use them here and now. "And what did you say?"

"I said with bells on."

My neck is tight, so I bend it to the side to stretch it out before grabbing the whiskey and pouring another drink. "Maybe you should wear red."

"I have the perfect dress."

"I just bet the fuck you do."

Isabella says, "Hardy." When I leave the fiery green eyes that are making my blood boil, I'm met with blues of no variation, no depth, and don't hold my interest. "That was rude."

"I'm sorry I don't live up to your standards. You're welcome to see yourself out."

She looks taken aback and hurt. "I don't know what's going on, but it's not like you to be rude like this."

"What do you know about me? Nothing. You're trying to rekindle a flame that I'm trying to blow out for good. Don't you get it, Isabella? We were done long before we broke up. So I don—"

She bursts into tears before my very eyes. *Whoa!*

I've never seen her cry. Not even when I broke up with her. And she's sobbing. Virginia wraps her arm around her, and says, "Come with me to the bathroom. We'll get you some tissues."

Now I burst out, but not into tears. "What the fuck is going on? No. You can't do that."

"What is wrong with you?" Virginia's voice is hard, not

familiar to me at all. The way she's looking at me makes me reel back. *Me? She's scolding me?*

"Is this rhetorical?" I ask because I'm truly unsure if she wants me to answer or not.

"You're being an ass, Hardy."

"You would know since that's what you like."

"Screw you." She walks away with Isabella.

And if I'm not totally mistaken, when Isabella looks back, I see that wicked evil grin of hers hidden beneath her fake sobs.

"Fuck me," I say, turning away.

Clive says, "Man that was tough to watch. I don't think I've ever seen anyone actually land and then get burned, but you managed to do just that. I thought you were in the clear, and then bam!"

"Okay. I get it. I'm fucked."

"Seven ways to Sunday, my friend."

I decide I need to make amends with Virginia and get Isabella out of my life for good. This whole scenario with her is feeling a little too reminiscent of our life together. I toss the towel on the counter and head for the bathroom.

My poor lamb was unknowingly led to the slaughter. Virginia comes out of the bathroom with Isabella behind her. Now it's V's tears that shine under the lights. I rush to her, but she pushes me away. "What happened?"

"You know."

"No, I don't."

"Don't play innocent, Hardy. If there's one thing I know about you, it's that you were never innocent." She starts for the door, but I take her arm.

"Wait."

"No," she says and yanks her arm free. "And about Saturday."

"What about it?"

She glances to Isabella who has stopped the dramatics long enough to enjoy the entertainment. "She told me what you said to her before I walked in. I know you were going to take her to your office."

"Choose your next words carefully, V."

"I don't have to be careful. The truth speaks for itself." She puts her jacket on and throws the gloves at my face. "Lowry asked me out for my birthday. I told him I had plans already, but I think I've changed my mind." One last look. One last hate filled look is given before she says, "Goodbye, Hardy."

I could argue with her all day, but we'll get nowhere with so much anger between us. So I turn mine to the woman who deserves it.

Isabella shrugs her pointed shoulders. "She has no strength or trust. A weak woman could never stand by your side."

"What did you tell her?"

"Nothing that you don't do any other night of the week."

"That woman," I say, sighing as my heart bleeds through my chest while shattering inside. "She's the only one I care about and you destroyed that. You destroyed the goodness that she had inside her."

"Hardy, we could be so good together again."

My emotions go numb, my heartbeats dull. My gaze hits her, and disgust returns. "Get the fuck out of my bar, and stay out of my fucking life."

"You don't mean that."

"I'm done." With Isabella. With love. With everything.

I walk away, leaving the blonde behind me just where she should have always stayed—in my past.

Chapter Twenty-One

Standing at the window of my apartment, I stare out. I can't see beyond two feet. The snow is dense. The weatherman has called it a blizzard and told his viewers to hunker down. But there's no hunkering to be done. The weather outside matches the storm raging inside me since Virginia walked out of the bar.

It's her birthday and I'm stuck inside during the snow-pocalypse. The bar is closed like almost everything else in Brooklyn. I have a feeling Manhattan is even worse. That's left me with nothing to do but relate to the bad conditions. Feeling sorry for myself has become my specialty over the last forty hours. Not that I'm counting. I've done everything to get a hold of her and she's just not having any of it.

Texted.

Called.

Email.

Pigeon carrier.

Okay, no pigeons were harmed in the process of getting a hold of Virginia. Nor were they used in any way, but if you know of any fanciers, let me know. Asking for a friend.

Bet you didn't know a bird handler was called a fancier. Well neither did I, but considering how much time I've spent alone in this apartment the last—looking down at my watch—forty and a half hours, Google has become my friend.

Sitting down on my rolling desk chair, I cruise back to the window and kick my feet up on the sill. Isabella sure did a number on my life. Like a tornado, she came. She destroyed everything in her path, and then fizzled back out. Now I'm left with a big disastrous mess to clean up and I have absolutely no idea where to start.

Two rotations on my chair later, I sit up and pull my phone from pocket. I'm going to try one more time. If she doesn't answer I won't be able to avoid her not so subtle hints anymore. If she doesn't answer this time, it's time to move on without her. It rings three times before it goes to voicemail, my heart sinking even lower. I hear the message that I've become too familiar with, "Hi, this is Virginia. Sorry I missed your call. Leave a message after the beep or if we're friends or family, text me instead because I hate checking voice messages." She laughs at her own joke, and I smile because I miss hearing it. "Take care. Bye."

The beep is heard, and I stall because I want to lay my heart on the line like I did for my parents the other day, but she's not even texting me, much less talking to me. "Happy birthday, Virginia." I'm not sure what else to say and I'm sure while I'm having this massive debate, it's getting creepier to listen to the silence as it spreads, so I just say, "I miss you."

I hang up and set the phone down. It rings and I jump, answering as fast as my heart races. "Hey."

"Are we staying closed tonight?"

Not the voice I was hoping to hear. *Romeo.* "Yeah. It's not safe for people to be out. I don't want to encourage it."

"All right," he says, and I can tell he has a smile on his face. "I'll just stay in bed the rest of the day." I think I hear kissing noises.

Fuck my life. "We're open the day after Christmas."

"Cool."

"Don't be late. Bye." I disconnect the call as quickly as I can before I'm stuck listening to him have sex with whomever he's with.

Sex.

Sex.

Sex.

Man, do I miss it. Why did I stop doing it? It's not like I didn't have a ton of offers over the last three or four weeks. Virginia didn't stop crushing, as she calls it, on that asshole lawyer, so why did I stop hooking up? Missed opportunities. Some lost, some are like a bar tab the women leave open, hoping I will finally say yes.

Maybe that's what I need. I need to say yes. I'm damn moody these days and that's probably not helping. I know my hand isn't. Righty takes the edge off of Big Richard, but he's never truly satisfied like he is after good hard fuck. Picking my phone up again, I scroll through some numbers. It's snowing hard. Everyone is home because the city has closed down. I've got my pick of the pretty kitties tonight, so whom should I choose?

***There never was a choice. As much as I don't like liars, I had become one of the best. When I finally started telling myself the truth, there was nowhere else I could go.

Trudging through the snow, the blizzard blinding my way at some points, I would be there for Virginia. Friend, foe, lover, despite the snow, I would go. I couldn't resist the rhyme, but at least it has reason. Being cold like this makes you loopy so I was reciting rhymes and the presidents again, but this time, not to keep my dick down. The freezing temperatures were doing a good job of that, but to keep my mind sharp.

No taxis.

No buses.

No subways.

No bikes.

No pedicabs.

Nothing. Nothing but a pair of snow boots with three pairs of socks underneath, those too tight on the three amigos down below, long johns, jeans, and waterproof jogging pants. I had so many shirts on, a college sweatshirt, and my coat that I looked like the Stay Puft Marshmallow Man. The scarf, hat, gloves, and earmuffs just added to the sexy I wasn't pulling off at all. But this isn't about looks or sex, but I see how you might have thought that this whole time. Nope, it wasn't about those things at all. They're shallow pursuits and something I pursued often—PMV.

After three hours, I'm finally standing in two feet of unplowed snow in Lower Manhattan solid in the conviction that the only thing I want to pursue is Virginia Ryan. Continuing my journey to her Mecca, I see a beacon of hope up ahead. My pace picks up and when I approach I look in through the window. It's not a mirage. It's real. And it's open. *Coffffeeeeeeeeeeeeeee.* Get in my belly and warm my bones. There's a line because apparently New York has a lot of other dumbasses like me who disregard weather warnings and still venture out. But maybe they're trying to work their way to the women of their dreams too. Fine. I take it back. They're not dumbasses. They're just in love. Which is kind of similar when you think about it too long. I choose not to and step up to order a coffee instead.

After placing my order, I step off to the side to check emails, texts, and hoping to have heard from her. I haven't. She's off fucking the asshole, giving up something she used to value all because I made her feel cheap. Yup, me. Not Isabella. She was a catalyst to the catastrophe, but it comes down to me. I didn't tell Virginia how I felt. I didn't tell her that I don't want to be with anyone else. I didn't tell her I stopped fucking around the night I started fucking around with her. I didn't tell her to be with me instead of Lowry.

And I should have.

Not because she's a chick and chicks need to hear it, but because it's the truth. My truth and that holds more coffee than this sixteen-ounce cup. I take the bag with the treat I bought and head back out into the snow.

Four more blocks and I finally make it to her building. Barry opens the door, tips his cap, and says, "Did you brave the elements alone?"

"For too long," I reply not referring to the weather. "I'm hoping to change that." I step inside the lobby. The lights are dimmer than usual, letting the holiday lights on the tree and around the desk shine brighter.

Stepping behind the tall counter, his gaze goes down, his eyes looking anywhere but at me. "Ms. Ryan isn't here right now."

There's this sickness, this ball that grows when I think about Virginia and the asshole together. I know she cancelled with me saying she was going to meet him, but that stupid little emotion named hope has stayed the course with me, hanging out in the most unlikely of places—my heart—since she walked out. I don't know. Maybe I was naïve to think she wouldn't go through with it. She doesn't owe me anything. Not her heart, nor her virginity. But damn it, that doesn't mean I didn't want both. I'm a guy for fuck's sake.

But if I can't have the latter, I want the former and I'll take it without hesitation. Her heart's what matters. I can't give her the other so if she goes through with it with the asshole, I'll still be here just like I promised.

Resting my hands on the counter, I ask, "Do you mind if I wait?"

"Not at all, Mr. Richard."

"Hardy."

"Hardy," he repeats with a tight expression that shows me he knows what's up. "Bourbon?"

"What?"

He holds up a flask. "If you'd like, I've got something that might take the edge off."

"I could use something to warm me up."

"Edge, not the chill, but it will do a good job of both."

"That obvious, huh?"

"That and that you're here in the middle of a blizzard and she's out there. Missed connections." He hands me the flask.

I take a shot. It's the cheap shit, but I'll take it. After one more gulp, I give it back. He follows with a shot of his own. I start to say, "I think I'm in lov—"

His hands go up. "Sorry, Hardy. I'm a doorman, not a bartender. Save your troubles for someone who can give you good advice."

"I'm a bartender."

Nodding, he laughs. "You're screwed then. If you don't have the answers, the rest of us are screwed too."

"I make cocktails." I lean against the counter. "I don't solve the worlds problems."

"Seems you can't solve your own either."

"Give me that flask."

He pulls it back out from under the desk and hands it to me. While I drink, he says, "I'm twice divorced and just got dumped last week. I'm not so keen on the love story anymore."

Putting the cap on the steel bottle, I give it back and then take my gloves off. "I never was and then . . . it just kind of hit me."

"Blindsided," he adds, nodding.

"Yeah, like a tackle to the heart."

"But more violent."

I chuckle. "Guess we'll see on that one. But I'm here."

"In a snowstorm no less."

"Ready to see if we even have a story."

"It's not about the story, the hows, whys, or wheres. It's about the ending. This is your chance to write the ending you want."

He's right. Like the bourbon, he's hitting me right in the feels.

***Barry's drunk. He's been on the phone for the last forty-five minutes with his girlfriend. At one point he told her, "I don't want caviar. I'm happy with fish sticks . . . No, not that you're fish sticks. I didn't mean that. I meant I love you. Let's go to Atlantic City for New Year's and get married."

He's gone and done it now. Scrubbing my hands over my face, I stand. It's after eight. The sun never came out and the pitch black of a sunshine-less world settled in. I try not to think it's an omen, but Virginia's still not home. That little doorstopper of hope that was holding my heart wide open for her has begun to slide closed.

Picking up my scarf, I wrap it around my neck and slip

on my coat. I put my gloves on and walk to the desk. "I guess I'm gonna go."

He says into the phone, "Let me call you back, Dolores . . . I will. Right back. I love you too." When he hangs up, he comes around and stands at the door. No one has come or gone for hours, much to his delight and the detriment of my idea of this great reunion. He turns to me. His eyes are glazed, his hat left back at the desk. His top button is open and his gloves are off. "You can't get far in this weather, at night."

"I'll get a hotel the next block over."

We both stand there, staring through the glass. There seems to be a small break in the snowfall, so I take the opportunity to leave. "Will you tell her I stopped by and give this to her?"

He takes the bag from me. "I will."

Patting him on the back, I say, "Congrats on the engagement, and thanks for the bourbon."

"You're welcome, Hardy. Happy holidays."

I pull on my hat, and when he opens the door, I walk back into the cold, dark night. "Happy holidays."

The door is closed and I head back the way I came. There's no traffic and fewer people out, but it's peaceful even if my heart is in turmoil. I lower my head when the snow starts up again. Crossing the street, I keep walking, thinking about what I'm going to order from room service. I'm starving after the trek I've done—my body physically exhausted and my mind emotionally tired. At the corner, I try to decide which way to go to the closest hotel.

"Hardy?"

Looking up, standing not even ten feet away is the most beautiful woman I've ever laid eyes on. My heart starts to pound, trying to reach her. "Virginia."

She stands there, and with each tentative step I take, her face comes into focus. Black lines streak her face, wet hair sticking to her forehead. She's got no hat and no gloves. She's got no sweet pink to her cheeks that I've always loved. But she carries something stronger in her eyes, something devastating, something that stops the pounding in my chest, and shatters my heart. When I reach her, she starts to cry, and says, "I'm so sorry."

Chapter Twenty-Two

I once knew this girl.

Pretty. So pretty it hurt sometimes.

Smart. Whip smart and clever. She always kept me on my banter toes.

Shy with the world, but *bold* with me.

It wasn't that long ago that I met her, only a month or so, but long enough to know. This is not that same girl before me.

I close the gap and wrap my arms around her as tight as I can. Her jaw is chattering and she's freezing cold. Her body is wracked with sobs as if she's held in a lifetime of pain. "We need to get you inside."

When I start to turn, she frantically grabs for my arms. "Hardy, I'm so sorry. I'm sorry."

Holding in my own lifetime of chaotic emotions that's built up since the day I met her, I run my thumbs over her cheeks, wanting the black gone from her sweet face. Then I reach into my pocket and pull out her gloves. I thought she'd be happy to have them but she bursts into tears again. "Why are you so nice?" she asks, her tone tingeing on anger. "I don't deserve it."

She slips the gloves on and I take my beanie off and pull it down on top of her head, making sure to cover her ears. "Let's talk about that when we're inside. You'll be sick if we stay out here much longer." She concedes with a nod. I wrap my arm around her and we walk back to her building.

We're greeted with a mile wide drunken smile. "Merry Christmas Eve, Ms. Ryan. Hardy, good to see you found what you were looking for."

"It took a while and I made a few detours, but it's good to finally reach my destination."

He rushes behind the counter to get something. When he reaches us at the elevator, he hands them to us. "Here's a tissue for you, Ms. Ry—"

"Virginia. Please call me Virginia.

With a smile that borders on permanent, he hands me the treat bag from the coffee shop. "You can give it to her yourself now."

"Thanks, Barry. I appreciate it."

"You're welcome. May I suggest both of you stay indoors and ride this storm out."

This is where I'm going to need a whole helluva lot of credit. I couldn't have asked for a better setup. But even I know there's a time and place and this isn't the time or the place.

Virginia's eyes meet mine, and she asks me, "Will you stay, through the storm?"

Taking her hand in mine, I lean down and kiss her cheek. "We can weather the storm together." The doors to the elevator open, and we step on. "Good night, Barry."

"Good night."

She moves closer and leans her head on my arm, our

hands clasped together. We both stare at the counter as the floors tick by. Every swallow is thick and loud and I know she can feel my heart beating unsteady, unsure of where we are, and what's to come for us.

On her floor we still hold hands until we're inside her warm apartment. The door is locked and we strip off the heavier layers. No one is breaking the quiet moments that weave between us, both of our nerves showing in our unease. She turns, but I take possession of her hand again, and stop her. "Hey?"

Her eyes fixate on me, the questions there.

"You're cold," I add. "Come with me."

Like me, she's either too tired or too cold to fight, and she follows without argument. Turning on the shower, I make sure to turn on the hot water. She stands behind and if I didn't know better, I could swear her gaze smacked my ass a few times as she ogled it. Catching her in the act, I say, "See something you like?"

She laughs until a dark guilt settles into the sound and with a sigh, she says, "I don't deserve you or your forgiveness."

"Sure you do. I'm a very forgiving person." I lean against the wall close to her and I hate that I need to know, but I need to know the full story for when I'm taken into interrogation over the murder of the asshole for hurting her. "I don't like holding grudges. I like to move on, so let's move on together. Get in the shower. It will warm you up and then tell me what I need to forgive you for?"

When she doesn't move, I turn my back. "I won't peek."

I can't hear her clothes coming off. Two weeks ago I would have never given her this courtesy. I'm a fucking perv sometimes. But now, with all that's happened, I'm willing to give her the space she needs if it means we can write a different ending to our story.

The shower door is closed, the frosted glass protecting her from peeping Hardy eyes. A moan is heard, and then she says, "This feels amazing. God, I thought I would freeze out there."

Flipping the toilet lid down, I sit. "I'll make you something to eat when you get out."

"You know what would make this even more amazing?"

"What?" The door cracks open and I'm starting to recognize the girl I know, the one that smiles at me like she's doing now, making each heartbeat feel heavy with the insta-love the hipster told me about.

"If you joined me."

I'm not sure if she even finished the sentence before my pants hit the floor. Her eyes go wide. "Compression pants?"

"I wear them in the cold, under my real pants."

"I totally get that. I'm just impressed that even when you're compressed like a sausage in a casing that you're so . . ." She points. "Well endowed."

"You had me at well endowed, V. Move over. I'm coming." Mind. Gutter. Yup. It's that easy for me to go there. Climbing out is a whole other case though. Standing next to her naked, if this is forgiveness, I'll give it to her by the well-endowed loads. Ew. That's not what I meant. Forget about it. "In."

The space in here is not as roomy as mine, another downfall of modern design—efficiency. But I want to thank the architect personally right now. It's not awkward. She just takes my hand and pulls me close, and I like close with her. While the water rains down on our bodies, she says, "You haven't asked because you're nice like that, but for the record, I'm still a virgin."

Angels voices are heralded from the heavens, "The Rifle Regiment" is trumpeted from the battlefields of my heart, and "Best Day of My Life" starts playing in the jukebox of my head.

Beyond Big Richard standing at full salute, wanting her those ways that I forgot to look up for legality purposes, I try to play off how happy I am. "Oh that's a bummer."

"What?" She leans back in surprise. "You're not happy?"

"No, I meant . . . I'm thrilled, fucking thrilled, but I don't know if I'm allowed to be happy without it coming off that I'm damn happy that I might still have a chance."

The warmth of her gaze and the brightness of her smile melt me on the spot. I recognize that look. I used to think she had hearts in her eyes, and that she was one good roll in the hay away from falling in love. It's not what I see, it's the torch I carry for her reflecting back at me. "You want a chance with me?"

I run my hand over her shoulder and rest it on the curve of her neck. This is it. This is my shot of owning that truth I've been living with since we met, the one that if she feels the same becomes the heavy weight champion for new best day of my life. The day I closed on the bar has been my reigning best for years now. It gave me the freedom to be who I wanted to be, to change the course of my life for the better, and lead me to standing in this shower stall with the most beautiful woman in the world, it deserves the title. This is my shot to not just be honest with her, but with myself. "I'm in love with you, Virginia Ryan."

Her eyes go wide. "Oh my God, you are?"

Damn, I didn't predict that reaction. Stepping away, my back hits the cold tile wall and I run my hands through my hair. "Umm . . . yeah, I was hoping you felt the same." Ugh.

This day just beat out when I was fourteen and my sister found out I had stolen my grandmother's Suzy Chapstick fitness book. She sold me out when she discovered some of the pages were stuck together. My mom pretended it was normal to talk about masturbation at the dinner table. My dad talked about hair on the hands and frostbite, or maybe it was how to handle blue balls. I forget now. But I will never forget that no one ate the hotdogs we had for dinner and that it was the worst day of my life. *Until now.* "This is so embarr—"

"No," she says, moving against me and teasing my dick with her incredibly slick and sinful body. "I do too." I dig my gaze up from where I'd just buried my heart at her feet and look into her vibrant greens. "I'm in love with you too, Hardy."

I drop another silver dollar into my mind's jukebox and "Best Day of My Life" starts back up. I'll be putting it on permanent rotation on my phone, changing my ringtone, and buying tickets to see American Authors as soon as I get home. "I thought you were in love with that asshole."

"I had a stupid crush on him, but I fell in love with you." That sweet pink is back and it's not from the hot water, but from me. Yep, this guy. I even pop the *P*. I'm owning that shit. That sweet pink is mine. All mine, and I've never felt happier about being pussy whipped. If it means I get to wake up next to Virginia every morning and go to bed with her each night, I'm in. I'm the whippiest of whipped.

I could say this is where I lifted her into my arms and carried her to bed, making sweet love to her on her birthday. You know, me as her gift. I've been told I'm quite the catch, after all. But that's predictable. So I kiss her once, then again. And then her fantastic tits, because holy Jack fucking Daniels I'm kissing Virginia Ryan's tits.

But we've waited this long, so we soap up and wash our hair, then I make her come so hard that Barry calls up to make sure she's okay. That's a lie, but it sounds more impressive than she practically collapsed in my arms from losing control of all the tension she'd been carrying. *Hrm* . . . maybe that does sound pretty damn good and since it's the truth, that's the story I'm sticking with.

By eleven, I have her waiting on the bed with the lights out. I light the candle and walk into the bedroom singing Happy Birthday really fucking loudly. I sound terrible, so I have a theory that if you sing at the top of your lungs people give you a pass on the sound of your voice.

Sitting on the end of the bed, I hold the cupcake forward, and say, "Make a wish, Virginia."

She blows out the candle. "You're here. I don't need anything else."

Leaning forward, I kiss her. Her hands cup my face, she kisses me again, and then says, "Actually, I do have one wish."

"What's that?"

Her request is my specialty. We've moved into the main part of the apartment and she's sitting on the other side of her bar—topless because that was my end of the deal. It was only fair since I'm shirtless and pantless. Since we're dealing with fire, she let me wear my boxer briefs. I toss the bottle into the air and catch it behind my back, whip it around and turn the cap, filling the glasses quickly. One twist. Two. When the orange garnishes are added to the whiskey, I get the lighter. "You ready?"

She nods excitedly, her eyes wide as she lifts up to get a good view. "It's so sexy how you handle those bottles."

"Wait until I handle you."

"I've waited my whole life for it."

"You know I'm a sure thing, right?" I ask, reminding her again. Lowering the lighter to the drinks, the fruit oil lights just how it's supposed to. Virginia squeals in delight, and I pop my imaginary collar. Two quick puffs and the flames are out and I hand her drink to her. "Taste the smokiness. It magnifies the liquor, which is why you should always drink the good stuff."

With her eyes closed, she savors the cocktail. I used to think cocktails were aphrodisiacs. They're not. She is. Fuck, I'm hard. I think I'll savor her all night long.

Dean Martin begins crooning "I've Got My Love to Keep Me Warm." I hold my hand out to her. "Dance with me."

She takes it and I walk around, joining her in the living room. Pulling her close, I try to get as much of her body against mine. Snow is still falling outside, but inside—it's warm and cozy. Leading with one hand, and the other on her lower back, we begin swaying to the music. She asks, "Will you go with me to the holiday party? We can party hardy."

"Did you just make a punny?"

"I did," she replies proudly.

"Well how can I possibly say no to that?"

"You can't. Can you get a tux on such short notice?"

"I own one, so I'm good."

Looking up at me, she says, "Why do I feel like there's so much more to learn about you?"

"Good thing we have a lifetime ahead of us."

"Be careful, Mr. Richard. I'm starting to see hearts in your eyes."

"I don't want to be careful anymore. Careful lost us time. I don't want to lose anymore with you."

Her forehead drops to my chest and she sniffles, so I ask, "What's wrong, V?"

She sniffles again, and then says, "You. This. It's all so perfect." Looking into my eyes, she grimaces. "I left tonight to spite you." I don't say anything. I can tell she needs to get this off her chest. "I was going to meet him to hurt you."

"What happened?"

"I got two blocks away and realized I didn't want to see him. I wanted to see you. So I was going to walk to Brooklyn, but I got caught in this gusty area and lost my hat. And I didn't have gloves because I had thrown them at you. I found a diner open and sat there warming up. I think I had three cups of coffee, but really I was thinking about what was happening between us."

We part and she takes a blanket and wraps it around her. Sitting on the couch, I lift my arm. She curls into my side, and continues, "Katie O'Dowd told me you were a lost cause, that many had tried to hook, line, and sinker you, but you were going to remain a forever bachelor. You were so determined to stick to the lesson plan that I thought if I told you I was falling for you that you'd end the lessons and wouldn't want to see me anymore."

"I was only doing those damn lessons to spend more time with you." She sighs, and I sigh with her. "We're quite a pair." I rub her arm, and ask, "Would you have gone through with the plan on New Year's if we hadn't had that fight?"

"I felt some pressure like I'd let you down if I didn't, but I wouldn't have. Until Isabella told me I had interrupted your time with her. Then I was determined to get rid of my virginity come hell or high water with Lowry."

"I'm sorry about Isabella, that she said those things to

you. It's not true. I had comforted her because she's going through a divorce. I should have known better."

Angling up to face me, she smiles. "I know someone we can set her up with."

"A match made in asshole hell?"

"Something like that." Her hand snakes over my abs and starts going lower. "By the way, did you say yes or no to New Year's Eve?"

Covering her hand, the pressure feels too good. My breath comes harsher through my nose, and I say, "Wouldn't miss it for the world."

"So can we say I love you anytime we want now that it's out there in the universe?"

"I'm counting on it." Lifting her up and onto my lap, I kiss her. When she opens her eyes, I say, "I love you."

"I love you, too, but I have another question."

"Ask away."

"Do I still get lesson four, the final lesson?"

Flipping her down on the couch beneath me, I say, "I'll be giving you the final lesson all right and then I'm going to test you over and over and over again." My hips move between her legs.

Her laughter punctuates the point I'm trying to make, and by point I mean we grind together until laughs turn to moans and I've given her the second gift of the night. *What can I say?* I tried to be humble but I'm an arrogant bastard, the king of orgasms, and as of tonight, Virginia Ryan's boyfriend—my most distinguished title to date.

Chapter Twenty-Three

It is official.

We are official.

Despite a blizzard of epic portions, a girl too stubborn to see what was right in front of her, and a very handsome, some might even call him debonair, man who foolishly believed he had a say when it comes to matters of the heart, we did it. *Not that.* Unfortunately, we haven't had sex yet. All for good reasons, but I'll come back to that. I happily traded in my bachelor card for one lovely Ms. Virginia Ryan.

Seven days ago, we made an agreement to put this lesson plan and asshole business behind us. It's worked out well for me. The weather is my friend, a supporter of love, and what I might have cursed that night, is now my ally. Since the storm grounded all flights, Virginia was stuck with me on Christmas. *Game point to Richard.* Her family was disappointed they didn't get to see her, but they were thrilled to meet me on their video call. They had no choice. We were trapped in her apartment for two days. *Match goes to Richard.* Our Christmas gift to each other was easy—

Hallmark movies, *her choice*. In bed, *my choice*. Naked. *Both of our choices*.

How we didn't seal the deal is beyond my comprehension. *Game point to Ryan*. I've never had to wait to be with a woman. I've always dated women who were more than happy to lead the charge right into bed. What I've discovered is that I don't need someone to lead the charge or to make it easy. I need Virginia. *Match goes to Ryan*. I need something that was real, something that I want for more than a few hours of fun. I want love. Not for just a few days, and when I look over at her sleeping soundly next to me, years comes to mind. *Ladies and gentleman, Ryan and Richard have met their match—Winners all around*.

Not to sound too sentimental, but she makes me want to break out in song and dance on the regular, and you've heard my theory on singing. Well, my dancing is okay. I know you thought I'd say something charmingly self-deprecating, but I have a few moves that might make Channing Tatum jealous. That's a lesson for another day.

Love.

It's all that matters. It controls almost all my thoughts and I look at life differently. It's all consuming, heart filling, blood rushing. It's magic for the soul, and we've got it in spades.

So when it comes to V's V-card, she's pounced me more times than I can count. It's like that thing is burning a hole in her pocket she's so anxious to spend it. It's been a real damn feat keeping her off my junk. Big Richard has seen so much hand action that I needed lotion for the chaffing. On the bright side, cuz yeah, me getting off can't really be on the dark side, it's not me doing the work anymore. She's become a sexual goodwill ambassador and my dick is the beneficiary. A sexual animal feeding for the first time with me as her prey.

Just last night I showed up at her place and within minutes, I was handed a beer "to sit back and relax," then she proceeded to pin me to the window, the little minx, while she rubbed on the outside of my jeans. I drank that beer because it was damn refreshing, so was my view of the woman in front of me. Eye to eye with Big Richard, she looked up at me, and said, "Take your pants off. This job isn't going to blow itself."

I'm not gonna lie, beer spewed everywhere. But the shower we took more than made up for the fact that I was now dating myself in female form. Hot in some ways, mouthy and a lot cocky in others. But I digress . . .

When it comes to lesson four, it isn't about the sex anymore. I'm a sappy sucker for love now. I even wrote Hardy hearts Virginia in the fogged up glass at the coffee shop two days ago. Luisa treated me to coffee, recognizing the old Hardy Richard is a thing of the past, and this new lovesick version is here to stay.

So when she finally does get that V-card stamped and turns it over to the sex commission, it has to be special. It has to be worth waiting all these years for. Fortunately, I'm the man with a plan. The man for her job. I'm on it, and plan to be in it, kissing it . . . you get the drift. After all, we're #MFEO.

***

New Year's Eve is booming in the hospitality sector. Running a popular business during the second biggest holiday for a bar means we were booked six months ago for a private party.

All the guys are working tonight—Romeo has a small audience of ladies hanging on his every cock tale. Clive is tossing bottles into the air and entertaining the crowd *Cocktail* style with flaming drinks. Leo has hit his stride and fits right in. He's a solid tender, and has a regular clientele, including the fashion icon, Vittori, which brings the bar more press. Eddie has everything under control—the ladies, the liquor, and the party. I knew he was ready to take on the job.

As for me, that's my name above the door, that one that shines on the glass. That means I get to cut out early and meet my girl just in time to kiss her under the midnight mistletoe.

I make my rounds and wish everyone a Happy New Year, including some of the ladies I used to spend private time with. Virginia has caused this goofy grin and I can't seem to get it to go away. I don't fight it too much. It kind of says everything about how I'm feeling these days, much to the ladies' chagrin. But we always had an understanding, so even though I'm off the market, they wish me the best of luck. They also tell me to keep in contact, but I've already deleted that contact list from my phone.

I wasn't even bothered by deleting the numbers. I rarely used them anyway, but when I looked my sweet girl in the eyes and we committed to this relationship, it needed to be fully. Virginia has a jealous streak. I don't want to feed the beast when she has nothing to worry about.

I receive a few catcalls and compliments when I'm leaving. Stealing Barry's move, I tip my imaginary hat and rush out to catch a cab. At this stage, karma even thinks I deserve some nookie. I've been a very good boy this year and plan on being extra naughty tonight.

Yep, karma's on my side when I'm able to get a taxi right away on one of the craziest nights in New York. "The Waldorf-Astoria, please."

"Traffic's bad. Just letting you know ahead of time."

I hand him a fifty. "If we can cut some time off, that would be great."

"I know some detours."

Leaning back, I check my phone. There's a text from my mom: *Your dad has been fondling his balls for days. Should I be worried?*

Me: *What?*

Mom: *I bought some silver balls last time I was in the city that came in a cute Asian fabric covered box. I was told they would help spice up our love life. So far, he plays with them all day, instead of me.*

Me: *No. Not having this conversation. Happy New Year.*

Mom: *Happy New Year, Hardy. Dinner this Sunday. You're bringing Virginia.*

Me: *Yes, Ma'am.*

Next message is a photo from my dad with the message: *Your mother got me these hand massagers for Christmas. You manipulate them around your hands with your fingers. I think they're helping my arthritis. If you need a Valentine's Day gift for Virginia, you can find these cheap in New York.*

I'd bang my head on the plastic shield dividing me from the driver, but I don't want to catch some disease, so I reply to him instead: *Dad, those aren't hand massagers.*

His reply: *What do you mean?*

I'm not in the right state of mind to explain what Ben Wa balls are tonight. It's a Big Richard downer. I type: *I can't do this over text. Let's have a drink later this week. Come by the bar. Happy New Year.*

Dad: *Sounds good. Have a good night, son. Happy New Year.*

The driver pulls over, and announces, "The Waldorf-Astoria."

I pay the cabbie, and work my way through the hotel. When I find the party, I search the ballroom for a red dress, but come up short. I step farther in, and let my eyes adjust to the low lighting. In the middle of a room of traditional black tuxes stands my beautiful girlfriend in a holy-shit-that's-short-glittering-gold-dress with the red soled fuck me shoes, as if seeing her long legs wasn't enough of a fantasy fulfiller.

Her dress might be shiny, but my smile far outshines it. That's my girl. That's my sexy as all get out woman. I make my way through the party and through the sea of suits. I reach through the pack, and ask, "May I have this dance?"

When she turns, her smile is kilowatt bright. Her long, dark hair is pinned back on one side with gentle waves rolling down the other. She might be a champagne cocktail tonight, but she'll always be my Paloma. "Of course," she replies, taking my hand. The suits part for her and she's in my arms in an instant. My lips are on hers, a fiery passion ignited. My hands are on her ass, because why not stake the claim for her whole company to see. I swing her out and back again as a slow song begins to play. "I'm glad you're here."

"Me too." I lean in to whisper in her ear, "Nice dress. What there is of it."

"Thanks for noticing."

"Every guy in this room has noticed. There's no mistaking it anymore, V. You may be the only woman in your department, but you most definitely are not one of the guys." We spin slowly around and I look into the eyes I've fallen in love with. "You look gorgeous."

"Thank you, Hardy. You look pretty damn delectable yourself."

"Speaking of, how much longer did you want to stay?"

"It's not midnight yet. I thought we'd kiss as the clock strikes twelve and all that traditional stuff that couples do."

"I was thinking we'd do something else."

"I'm open."

"That's part of the plan."

A devious smirk accentuates her red lips. "I'm liking the sound of this plan. Should I say my goodbyes?"

I send her a wink. "You should definitely say your good-byes." Stepping back, I add, "Meet me at the elevators in ten minutes."

"I'll be there."

I could stand here all day, watching her sway through the crowd, but there's no way I'm missing this very important date. Screw the lesson plan, this is a date with destiny.

The elevator arrives just as she does. When we step on, she asks, "Your place or mine, big boy?"

"Mine," I reply, referring to the apartment and the girl.

Chapter Twenty-Four

Thirty minutes until midnight. The countdown is on and the door is open. I had only enough time to do the basics, but I think she'll like it. When we walk into the large apartment, her mouth drops open. "This is all yours?"

"Yes."

"You own the entire fourth floor?"

"I own the entire building."

She does a double take. "Guess I chose the right bartender then."

I chuckle. "Guess so, but I think fate had us locked up long before we met."

Walking around the empty space, she stops to look out the windows. Her hands press to the glass and she looks around at the neighborhood. She looks damn good taking up that real estate. When she turns back, she's smiling, but it's soft like her delicious curves. "You've always been quite the romantic."

"Only for you, V." I hold my hand out to her. "Come here. I want to show you something."

I lead her to the master bedroom. Just inside the doorway, she halts in surprise, a hand covering her mouth as her eyes get glassy. "Hardy."

"Virginia." I had to have a little fun.

"You did this for me?"

"Yes." I'm quite proud of myself. Finding a mattress company to deliver on the eve of New Year's Eve was tough, but that's what is so great about this city. You can find anything you want at any hour for the right price. Money talks. Fortunately I've got enough to hold the conversation.

She walks to the bed and sits on the fluffy blanket that matches hers. I thought it would make her feel more at home, more relaxed, and comforted. Battery-operated candles fill the floor along the far wall and I rigged some drapes into place this afternoon. I hate to be fucking blinded in the morning. And if all goes according to plan, we'll be sleeping late.

I have a bar cart set up with bottles of water, liquor, some snacks, and a bucket of chilled champagne. It's New Year's, which means celebrating, which means champagne. I pop the cork as she slips off her shoes. I want those damn shoes on, but I want her in bed naked more. "This place is beautiful and what you did in this room . . . Hardy, you've stolen my heart."

When I sit next to her, I say, "I don't want to steal your heart. I just want to be a part of it."

"You're more than a part. You own the whole entire thing."

We kiss and then toast, "To us." Simple. Sweet. And uncomplicated. Just like the woman before me. After we take a sip, I set the glasses on the floor, and cup her face. "I want to make love to you."

Her hands cover mine, and without hesitation, she says, "I want that too."

Languid lips become eager as I move my hand to the back of her head, holding her close. The fire ignited at the party flames the passion that's burning within. Kissing her is one of my favorite pastimes, but I wonder if it will be the victor after tonight. Our tongues touch, but our hands are tentative. I whisper, "I'll go slow."

"Okay." She doesn't use her inside voice, her nerves peeking through.

A kiss to the cheek, and then one to the neck. I run my hand over her dress and slide just inside the bottom hem. And then farther until we're both panting. When I don't reach any more material, my eyebrow matches lower extremities—shooting straight up. "No underwear, Ms. Ryan?"

"I was hoping to get lucky."

With a laugh, I say, "Let me know how that works out for you." I stand and bring her to her feet. While I work on removing the tux, she pulls her dress down, finding a new place for it to live, right next to my jacket and her shoes. The temptress winks at me. "So far. So good."

"You're telling me." Her oh so criminally dangerous body climbs under the covers and with her hands behind her head, she watches me undress. Without apology and no nerves in sight, her eyes roam my body and her bottom lip is bit.

Finally, I have all the pieces off and get under the covers with her. Instead of something sexual, which is more my M.O., seeing her here and just being with her, I say, "I'm glad you're here."

The ease is seen in her smile when she replies, "So am I."

Maneuvering closer, I kiss her again, letting her linger on my lips. I move lower kissing a wet trail down between her breasts and stopping to swirl my tongue in her belly button.

When I reach the sweetness between her legs, she's already gripping the sheets. "You don't have to do that, Hardy. You've been more than patient with me."

I look up, resting my hands on her hips. "I'm in no hurry, Virginia. I can wait until you're ready."

"I'm ready. I don't want you to feel obligated to do all this for me. You don't."

"Who says it's only for you?" A smile rolls in, and my job here is done. Oh wait, now I smile because we're just getting started.

"I might have just fallen more in love with you."

"Well hang onto your heart because it's about to get a whole lot swoonier in here." I not only spell the presidents' names, with my tongue to her clit, but within minutes she's screaming mine. And just fuck, that's so damn hot.

The moment of truth happens differently than I thought it would go down. Or up depending on how you position yourself. Anyway, I've got this gorgeous girl lying naked on the bed waiting for me to teach her everything I know about sex. No pressure or anything.

"It doesn't work like that," I say, rolling the condom down my cock.

She watches with the same intensity she expressed while reading the *Mathematical Principles of Natural Philosophy* by Isaac Newton. She's got the most astute quest for knowledge. Of all sorts apparently. "Why not?"

"Because it can be just physical and rough, pleasurable in that way. But with us, we have more at stake."

"We have our hearts on the line." She lies back, ready for me.

"Exactly." I position myself, getting a good feel for the situation at hand, or dick more accurately. When I'm settled snugly between her legs, I lean down and kiss her with my emotions as my erection kisses her while pushing in. "Good lord, Sweet Jesus." Names taken in vain come tripping from my mouth.

"What? What is it?" She sounds out of breath, and worried, and we just started.

Maybe I pushed too far the first time. Her nails start to dig into my shoulders, so I begin to move again—slowly. "You feel too amazing."

A smile crosses her face, and then I push all the way inside her. Her mouth falls open and her eyes fall closed. "Hardy," she releases my name on a sigh.

I open my eyes to see her, to watch as she experiences this the first time, much like how it feels for me. "Are you okay?"

"I've never felt like this. I feel full, like every minute that existed before was empty. You feel so amazing." The warmth of her hand spreads across my cheek as she caresses it. "Like you were always meant to be a part of me."

"Made for each other."

"Yes, like we were made for each other. Please start moving again though. I want more."

And so it begins . . .

Holding myself above her, I drop down low enough to kiss her while making love to her body, and what an amazing body she has. Her skin is smooth along her long legs, and I loop my arm under her sexy knee, bending it to my side. Her body is lean but soft in all the right places and

I begin to steadily thrust. Her hips join mine, engulfing me deeper.

I watch her reactions. My body's inner coil is tightening as Virginia's body embraces mine. She takes me into her supple haven and we move as if we were always meant to be together. "Are you okay?" I whisper, not sure if I've ever felt this lost to sensations before.

"So good, babe. Keep going. Don't slow down."

Smiling, our making love turns into a good fucking as she takes and gives, accepts, and returns the favor. Her nails digging into my skin spur me on to move even faster. I'm getting close, so close. I reach to where our bodies are joined and find her little erotic bundle of nerves. With my thumb, I put pressure where I know she wants it. "Can you come for me, baby?"

"Oh my God. I'm so close already. Harder." Her back arches and her head pushes into the bed, opening her body up to me like a flower blooming for the sun. "Keep going." A little more pressure sends her moaning and she let's go, falling into a bliss that strums through her like a string on a guitar. She's stunning in her orgasm as her body flexes around me, encouraging my own release.

Holding her by the shoulders, I fuck with all I have left, my body demanding I go big while heading into home. Darkness clouds my view and the lights burst, and I give in wholly to the demanding release. I collapse on top of her, and roll to the side, my soul sighing in contentment. "Holy—"

"Jack fucking Daniels."

A woman after my own heart. Through my haze, I smile, reach over, and pull her to me. One eye opens and then another. She's looking over at me with a huge, sassy grin on her face. "That good, huh?"

"Better than I hoped and I had high hopes considering I'm learning from the best."

"You're good for my ego, you know that." I lean over and kiss her head. "You're good for me."

"Will it always be this good, Hardy?"

"The sex? It will get better. Trust me."

She giggles, and hits my chest playfully. "I meant us, *this*, being together."

"This will get better too. You can trust me on that as well. I'll make sure of it." I yawn, and hold my arm above my heading, look at the time. "Twelve past midnight."

Popping up, she says, "We missed a kiss at midnight."

"Oh we were kissing at midnight, baby. And a whole lot more."

Settling back down and laughing lightly, she says, "You're right. We sure were. I can't believe you popped my cherry."

"Popped, tasted, devoured."

"Okay, enough of that. Let's just go with Happy New Year."

"Happy New Year." We kiss before she gets out of bed and hands me my glass of champagne.

"Cheers."

"Cheers." We sip and then I kiss her again just because I can.

She slips out of bed and goes to the bathroom. Watching her pad across my floor I can't help but hope to have this view more often. And I really fucking hope that my dad is right about what you are doing at midnight is what you'll be doing all year long because I could really get onboard with being inside V all year.

We swap turns and when I return to bed, I lay my head next to hers. My arm is holding her by the waist while my body relaxes, ready for sleep. Vanilla and sex lingers in the air, a smile lingering on her face. I give her a kiss and close my eyes. I'm not sure what comes over me, but I move even closer, molding myself around her.

Drawing figure eights on my arm, she already knows me, can feel that something's weighing on my mind. Her voice is soft like her touch. "Are you okay, Hardy?"

My head and heart are fuzzy. "I'm feeling a little drunk."

"I didn't think you drank much tonight."

"I didn't."

"Then how are you drunk?"

Opening my eyes, I whisper, "Since I met you I've been drunk on love."

She kisses my nose. Her tone is reassuring, her lips soft against my skin. "That's the best kind of drunk."

"I'm going to have one helluva hangover." I smile. "It might last years."

"I'm good with years."

Rolling on top of her, Big Richard is wide-awake again and ready for more. I can't deny his drive. He has the stamina of a stud. I try to calm him down but it's Virginia he's reacting to, so that's near impossible. When I look at her though, she has this amazing way of making the past not matter, the present really fucking sexy, and the future brighter. Happiness isn't on the horizon, I've found it and I intend to hold onto it. "How do you feel about a lifetime?"

The right side of her lips curls up. "Ask me tomorrow when you're sober."

"I will, and every day after."

"Be careful what you say next, Hardy, or you're gonna find yourself engaged and living in Connecticut." I chuckle.

"What about a fourth floor penthouse with a private elevator and rooftop deck?" "You have a rooftop deck?" Her excitement bubbles up.

"I do."

"Can we go up?"

"And here I was hoping we'd go down."

"You are so horny."

"Beats being an asshole."

"Good point, Mr. Richard."

"Speaking of sex—"

"We weren't talking about sex at all."

"You're right. Let's not talk about it. Let's do it instead."

A moan escapes her lips when my hand slips between her legs. While I fuck her with my fingers, I kiss her tits. *Now this is bliss.* This is happiness.

In the wee hours of the first day of the year, I'm lying in bed with V tucked in next to me. I used to think cocktails with a side of cock tales were the key to happiness, and that people only needed a good time and a great fuck to get by.

A virgin named Virginia changed my mind, my heart, my body, and my soul. Yup, she owns all of me. And I'm pretty sure I own all of the good parts that make her whole. *Go me!* With my free arm raised in the air, I do a silent cheer, careful not to wake her.

But like I've been known to do, let's give credit where credit is due, serendipity may have played a part in the Virginia and Hardy love story, but it was us who rewrote our ending. Together, we're living that happily ever after one great fuc—*eh*, you get the picture.

The End.

* * *

Looking for your next binge-worthy read? Check out the sneak peek of *Never Got Over You* by turning the page.

Never Got Over You

New York Times Bestselling Author
S.L. SCOTT

Cover Photographer: Regina Wamba of ReginaWamba.com

Cover Models: Claire + Noah Villalobos

Cover Designer: RBA Designs

Editing:

Marion Archer, Making Manuscripts

Jenny Sims, Editing4Indies

Proofreading: Kristen Johnson

Beta Reading: Andrea Johnston

Chapter 1

Natalie St. James

I'm the first to admit I have no business taking another shot.

Especially after the past two.

But what's a girl to do when a room full of strangers is chanting my name and a particularly wild best friend places the shot hat on my head along with a small glass of liquor in my hand?

I drink.

In a little hole-in-the-wall hidden from the main street in Avalon on Catalina Island, I down the liquid like a champ, then promptly proceed to fall from grace, also known as the barstool.

My eyes close, bracing for impact, except . . . someone catches me just before landing. With my breath caught in my throat, I hang in the balance of arms made of steel and open my eyes.

Laughter fades away with any drunken shame that threatened as I stare into the soulful eyes of a stranger.

"Hi," whispers the future hero of my dirty dreams . . . *oh, wait.*

Maybe I'm unconscious? Maybe I was knocked out cold, and I'm dreaming. I blink. Why are my eyes open? Letting my lids fall, I keep them closed long enough to pray, "Please let him be real. If he's not, I'm begging you to leave me in this dream a little longer." My lids drift back open to find him still staring at me.

"Are you okay?"

"Perfect," I reply. *I think.* I'm not sure if I actually voice the response or not. I feel pretty damn perfect in his arms, though, the response still fitting in any circumstance that involves me, him, and those arms wrapped around my body.

Naked would be nice, but I'll save that for our second date.

His brow furrows, but a smile curls the corners of his lips.

The fog of alcohol clouds my mind, creating a heavy blanket on my brain. Regardless, I try to calculate the odds of a ridiculously sexy stranger—the exact man I'd craft if Create-a-Hottie was an actual thing—being in the right place at the right time to catch me if I fell.

It's impossible, so the only logical answer to this conundrum is that either he is the best college graduation gift ever or I'm dreaming. "How are you so hot?" I ask, worried he'll disappear in a puff of smoke and mirrors. Clamping my eyes closed again, I whisper, "Dear Lord, please don't let him be a mirage."

"I'm real." *Yes!*

Does that mean my friend set up this encounter for me? She's always been a great gift giver. It is our job, after all. I squint one eye open, biting my bottom lip. "*Mm*, so real," I purr. *Too perfect to be real, though. I must be dreaming.*

His grin creates dimples that could compete with the Grand Canyon. *How did I know I liked dimples enough to add them into this delirium?* I don't know, but score one for me.

"I think you're going to be okay," my dream man says, his voice as delectable as his face.

Wait, what? No. "As for me being okay, not so fast, buddy. No need to rush toward the waking hours. Anyway . . ." I drape my hand across my forehead. "Dream or real, I'm going to need mouth-to-mouth resuscitation."

His dimples dig deeper. "Is that so?"

"*So* right," I pant.

"Do you think I should call a paramedic?"

"That's a little kinky for me, but if you're into it . . ." I press my lips into a pretty little pout to seriously consider this twist. "Nah. Changed my mind. I only want you. Just the two of us resuscitating each other."

"You want me?" he asks, surprise tingeing his tone as he cocks an eyebrow. He readjusts me in his strong, manly arms. "Circling back to the real part, you do realize you're not dreaming, right?"

I reach up and wrap my arms around his neck, wanting to melt in his arms again. Totally obsessed with how I fit so perfectly, I pull him closer and hold tight. "You do realize you're stupidly attractive, right?"

He chuckles, his grin lifting higher on one side.

That smirk would totally get me into bed, given what it's doing to me while dreaming. I close my eyes again. "I'm ready."

"For what?" His deep, dulcet tones vibrate through my body.

"Resuscitation. I'm ready. Resuscitate away."

When nothing happens, I peek one eye open. He's still

staring at me with the smirk I'm ready to kiss off his sexy face, and whispers, "I don't think you need me—"

"Trust me." Opening both eyes, I also run my fingers through his shiny, chestnut-hued hair, taking in the feel of the soft strands. "I really, *really* need you."

When he leans down, I prepare my lips with a quick lick before meeting his . . . or at least, that's the direction I hope this dream is going.

"I was thinking—"

"Yes?" My gaze floats from his mouth to his eyes again.

"We've been at this a while. Maybe we should get you off the floor?" His head tilts to the side, and the industrial lights above him shine bright in my eyes, almost like a place of business, a restaurant, or a bar would hang. My senses begin to return, starting with the stench of old beer scenting the air.

"Yuck." Next comes a wave of cedar-y cologne and salty air. That's a scent I approve of, but that's when something else hits me. *What if I'm not dreaming?*

"Up you go," he says, shadowing me again as he tries to lift me to my feet.

I don't budge. "Dream or not, I quite enjoy being horizontal with you."

"Are you always this, *should we say*, flirtatious?" he asks, laughter punctuating his question.

"Not when I'm awake, no."

As if he couldn't be more gorgeous, little lines whisker from the outer corners of his eyes, enticing me to drag my fingertip along each one. I don't, but I want to. "Are your eyes hazel or brown? It's hard to tell in this light."

"Brown."

"Brown does them a disservice. A kaleidoscope of colors

is trapped inside them. I'm going to need a closer look in the sunshine."

"The sun will be setting soon."

"Then we should hurry."

A restrained chuckle wriggles his lips. "You can stare into my eyes, but I have to warn you, once you do, you'll fall madly in love with me. And I'm leaving tomorrow, so if we're falling in love, you better get to the loving part since you've already fallen."

"Good point."

"Get up, Natalie," my best friend says, rudely barging into my fantasy and peering at me from beside his shoulder. "The floor is filthy! Now you're going to have to wash your hair."

My eyes shift her way. "Please go away and let me have this one little dream, Tatum."

Snapping her fingers twice in front of my face has me jerking my head back. "You're wide awake and making a fool of yourself."

Noise from the crowded bar filters into my consciousness. Instead of looking around to confirm, I stare into Dreamy's eyes a moment longer and then exhale as embarrassment becomes reality, returning me to the present. "You're real, aren't you?"

A slow nod accompanies a smug expression.

The heat of my cheeks has me pressing my hands to them in hopes of cooling my skin down. "Do you mind helping me up?"

"I need to know something first."

"What?" I ask, knowing I should leave before I'm sober enough to realize how absurd I've been behaving.

Still holding me in his arms as if I'm light as a feather,

he leans closer with his eyes on my mouth. When his gaze rises to meet mine, he asks, "Did you fall in love?"

My heart rate spikes, and the sound of it beating whooshes in my ears. Maybe I did hit my head because I swear at that moment, the one with my dream man so close I can kiss him or even lick him if I want, I can answer honestly.

Despite all the physical signs of me feeling otherwise, I reply, "You know. I think it's time for me to go." *Before the last few minutes really sink in.*

My feet are set on solid flooring while his hands remain on the underside of my forearms to steady me. Like the perfect gentleman. "I wish—"

"Nat," Tatum says under her breath. She moves in and grabs my hand.

"What?"

Her hair catches the light when she flips it over her shoulder, an exhausted sigh following right after. Every blonde needs a brunette bestie, and Tatum Devreux was destined to be mine since our mothers exchanged silver spoons from Tiffany's as baby shower gifts. I'm not exactly the calm to her wild ways, but she can out party me any day.

"A party on a yacht down in the harbor. We have to go now, though."

Panic rises in my chest. I know I should want to hightail it out of here to save myself from further mortification, but I don't want to go. I'm perfectly content right here.

I'm not shy about it. I look straight at him, but I'm smacked with a dose of candor I wasn't ready for, my ego crushed under his expression that mirrors pity. Now I regret not making a quick getaway when I had the chance.

My stomach plummets to the floor I was just hovering

above. "Yeah, it's time to go," I tell Tatum, my hand pressing to my belly in an attempt to keep myself together. My hand is grabbed, and I'm tugged after her as she calls, "Ciao, darlings."

I turn back to catch Mr . . . *Dreamy, Smug, Sexy, Pity-er of Drunk Girls* watching me. I'm left with two options to make an escape without further incident. I *could* blame the craziness on a head injury, or I *could* just leave. "So . . . thanks," I say awkwardly as I back toward the door. *Yes. Choosing the latter.*

"Are you sure you're okay?" His voice carries over the lively crowd.

I dust the dirt off my ass. "I'm fine. Guess I'm not a tequila girl."

"You drank rum," he replies with a lopsided smile that could sweep me off my feet again if I'm not careful.

"Rum. Tequila. Same difference." I wave off the idea because it doesn't really matter. "I'm not good with liquor." That should settle it, but I make the mistake of daring to look into his eyes again. The five feet between us virtually disappears, and mentally, I'm back in his arms again, reading the prose that makes up his features. It would take me days to interpret, capturing not only his thoughts but a history that's worn in the light lines. He makes it hard to look away.

Stepping forward, he raises his hand and then lowers it to his side again as conflict invades his expression. "You sure you're okay? You might have a concussion."

I can't say I'm not touched by his concern. Grinning, I ask, "Does a concussion involve my heart?"

"What's happening with your heart?"

"It's beating like crazy."

Smiles are exchanged. "I think you're experiencing something else, but if you'd like me to call an ambulance—"

"Nope," Tatum cuts in, yanking me toward the door again, and laughs. "He's cute, but we don't want to miss the yacht." She whips the straw hat off me and tosses it to him.

I twist to look back. "Thanks for the lift. *Literally.*"

"Anytime," he says with his eyes set on mine. When he shoves his hands in his pockets, he looks like he's posing for a Ralph Lauren ad. Tan. Rugged good looks. Tall. Those dreamy eyes and a grin that call me back to him. But life isn't a dream. It's time to return to reality.

Goodbye, dream man. It was nice hanging with . . . onto you.

Chapter 2

Nick Christiansen

Two days without the worries of late-night study groups, working my ass off interning at a law firm, and the constant micromanagement of my dad. At twenty-five, I've been ready to break out from under his thumb for a long time now.

He just hasn't received the memo that I'm not a kid anymore.

A last-minute invitation for a quick getaway before graduation from Stanford Law School and the pressures of my family brought me here. That's all this was supposed to be. A night of hanging with my best friend, a day of kicking back around the resort pool, and then barhopping to celebrate my final year of school behind me, today should have been much the same.

So, what just happened?

I know. Grinning as I recall how one minute, I was finishing my beer to the sound of spinning keys around my best friend's finger, and the next, chanting was filling my ears. *"Shot. Shot. Shot."*

I saw *him* first, an asshole ready to take advantage of an opportunity. The opportunity—a certain blonde in a loose white shirt, wide open between the top two buttons. Cutoffs reveal a lot of leg—shapely tan thighs—and a brown leather belt hangs around her waist more for decoration than for a purpose. Her sandals, only noticeable if you're looking for them, don't add any height. Bracelets of silver and gold with touches of turquoise covered her wrists, and the bar's raggedy shot hat had just been placed on her head. Clearly, I spent more than a few seconds taking her in without regret.

She was a vision in any state—from New York to California, drunk or sober—but it wasn't her outfit that had me acting on instinct and running into others to get to her. It was the asshole bragging about fucking her before she realized what hit her. Sure, I could have snapped back that no one would even know he was fucking her since he has a minuscule dick. But the hard lines of his face and the anger found in his dark eyes had me believing he meant what he said, not in jest or as a threat, but as a mission he intended to complete.

I should have punched him in the fucking face, but I didn't have time. I dashed the second my attention was grabbed by the sound of a squeal, the sight of arms in the air, and the pretty woman flying toward the floor.

Because I'm good with my hands, I've caught everything from the attention of college football scouts to a swordfish on vacation. I've also been called a golden boy my whole life growing up in the Golden State. But catching this girl right before she hit the floor might be my best catch yet.

She weighed nothing but made quite the impression. I

flexed my fingers under her back to rid myself of some weird energy burning through me. *God, I sound like my mom.*

I swore I'd never believe in that New Age stuff. She did her best to preach it, but logic has to play a part in our outcomes. But there's no logical answer as to why I'm still thinking about the woman I held for so long as if more was at play than two people colliding into each other's lives without their permission.

The back of Harrison's hand lands on my chest. "Nice save, but why'd you let her get away?"

"She's free to do as she pleases."

"What?" he asks, his brow careening between his eyes. "No, I mean, why didn't you get her number? She was hot, and the way you held on to her was like you had no intention of letting her go. It was becoming awkward watching the two of you cling—"

"We weren't clinging to each other. I was—"

Shaking his head, he says, "Save it, Nick. I don't need to hear about you falling for some chick."

"Technically, *she* was the one who fell."

"Let's not make this weird." He nods toward the door. "Taylor put us on the list. We've got to go before the yacht leaves the dock."

I follow him toward the door, but not without stopping by the asshole on my way out. "Today's your lucky fucking day because if we ever cross paths or you go within thirty feet of that woman again, you'll be flat on the ground before you know what hit you. Got it, fucker?"

He stands up but quickly realizes he has to look up to meet my eyes and sits back down. "Fuck off," he grumbles through a wiry beard.

My arm is caught before I have a chance to land a hit. "He's not worth it," Harrison says.

He's right.

This fucker also isn't worth a night in jail.

As the asshole cowers on the barstool with his head lowered, flinching from a hit that won't come, I lower my arm. "Lucky fucking day."

The conversation slowly resumes as Harrison and I head for the exit. My friend laughs under his breath just outside the entrance. "What gives, Christiansen? We haven't been in a fight in a long time." Cracking his knuckles, he adds, "Don't get me wrong. I'm up for it, but why are we fighting some guy twice our age in Catalina?"

"He needs a lesson in . . ." *Blonde. Tan. Blue-eyed beauty.*

"In what?" Harrison asks as he whacks me in the arm.

Ripping my gaze away from the blue-eyed beauty kneeling beside a scooter, I glance at Harrison. "Huh?"

When I return my attention to her again, I hear him grumble. "Ah. It's all so clear now."

I seize the moment. "This is a coincidence. Hi, again," I say, raising a hand while my voice pitches like a thirteen-year-old hitting puberty. *What the fuck?* Clearing my throat, I mentally berate myself for sounding like an idiot.

Harrison and both of the women turn to look at me. The blonde stands up with a reassuring grin on her face and shoves her hands into her back pockets. "Hi again, yourself."

I'm not the only one seizing the day. Harrison saunters up and asks her friend, "What seems to be the trouble?"

"Trouble with a capital T. Hi, I'm Tatum," she says.

Harrison takes her hand. "Pleasure to meet you. I'm Harrison."

Although she appears to blush, she pulls her hand and then points at the tire. "We have a party to get to, but we have a flat, and the rental company won't be here for an hour."

"That's quite the dilemma. Maybe we can help," Harrison says.

It's funny how he was in such a hurry not three minutes prior. He moves in to take a closer look. Harrison Decker was born with two trust funds and a gaggle of nannies. He didn't exactly grow up knowing his way around mechanics. I can't judge him too harshly since my background is similar, but I can still laugh at him because at least I know how to change a tire.

He leans back, glancing up at the brunette. She's pretty but doesn't hold a candle to the beauty beside me. Speaking of . . . I walk around the Vespa and lean down. Squeezing the tire, I listen. My eyes meet Harrison's, who's stepped off to the side with his new friend. His lack of loyalty isn't a surprise when there's a pretty woman around.

Her friend called her Natalie, but since we haven't been introduced, I just say, "You have a slow leak."

"Announce it to the world, why don't ya." She can't keep a straight face and cracks up. "Sorry, I had to."

I chuckle because of how much she makes herself laugh. She still waves it off. "Sorry, as you were saying." Another giggle escapes, though.

"The company shouldn't have put you on this scooter without checking it properly."

I look to my side to find those blue eyes staring into mine. "So we're stuck?" She grabs the tire, pumps it a few times like that might bring it back to life, and then drags her hand over a few treads. Leaning awkwardly on it, she adds, "Together?"

Is she flirting? It's not the approach I'd take, but it's curiously entertaining. "Afraid so." We both stand back up.

"You don't have to be afraid. I won't bite."

Something tells me she might by how her gaze darts down my body and back up again.

"I didn't mean I was actually afraid."

"I know. I was just teasing." If I didn't know she was drunk, I'd assume she was odd. She definitely has a quirky sense of humor. Maybe I do too because when she rubs her temple, she smears black grime along the side of her face, and I have to stop myself from laughing.

I reach forward, determined to help her out, but a spark fires in her eyes, and she says, "I knew we should have rented the golf cart. Tatum insisted on the Vespa, but I don't trust anything with less than four wheels."

"Wise." That response brings her earlier smile to the surface. "I heard your friend call you—"

"The party," her friend cuts in, wearing an expression scrunched with concern. "We're not going to make the party if we don't leave now."

"We can stay—"

"That's it!" Harrison snaps his fingers. "You can stay and help with the tire, and I can give Tatum a ride. Problem solved."

"A ride? Yes, that's great," Tatum says without missing a beat, already heading for the scooter with him in tow. He pats my shoulder on the way, the message already received loud and clear. *Guess I'm staying.*

"You don't mind, right?" Tatum asks as she slips on a helmet and swings her leg over the back of the Vespa. I'm about to answer, but the beauty next to me replies instead. "What about our girls' trip?"

"It's going swimmingly, don't you think?" Tatum points at Harrison and silently mouths, "He's so hot." For Harrison's ears, she adds, "We're turning lemons into lemonade."

The beauty next to me exhales and then frowns, her eyes reflecting her change in mood from the fun-loving girl I met inside. The sun shines in her eyes just before she rolls them. "Swell. All we need is vodka."

"Thought you didn't know much about alcohol?"

Rocking her hand back and forth, she laughs. "I'm no expert, but I've had a few lemon drops in my life." Looking right at me, she asks, "Have you had one before?"

"No."

"You should." It's as if she's forgotten about her friend altogether. "They're really good."

"Maybe we can get one together."

"Maybe." Her grin is sure and quite stunning. But that grease . . . I should really tell her about the smudge on her face, but it's sort of cute how unsuspecting she is of the mess.

Harrison backs out of the parking space and stops in front of me. "I'll see you back in the room."

"Yeah. Sure." I'm not bothered he's taking off with a chick. That's how we've always operated, not giving each other a hard time over a hookup.

Just as he pulls to the edge of the parking lot, Tatum motions to her friend's temple area, but then says, "I promise to make it up to you back in the city."

When they blend into traffic and travel around the corner, we're left in their dust. I'm more interested in the blonde next to me. She stares down the street with her hand as a sun visor and then shifts to the curb, sitting down on it. She laughs at some inside joke, then turns to me. "Guess you're stuck with me."

I sit down next to her. "There are worse people to be stuck with, I suppose," I reply, gently nudging her like we're old friends.

"You sure about that?" Her smile breaks through the disappointed façade she briefly tried on for size, the other one never quite fitting her natural disposition. Nor her drunk one. "For all you know, I could be a nightmare to deal with."

"I'm fairly certain I'll be okay. You're not a serial killer, are you?"

Offense colors her expression but is whisked away just as quickly. "*Me?*" Her fingers swirl near my nose. "I'm not the one with that boy-next-door face."

Capturing one of her fingers, I hold it hostage and grin at her. "You say that as if it's a bad thing."

"Handsome guys are always so cocky, too."

"All I heard was handsome."

I'm granted another front-row seat to an eye roll, this one more dramatic and aimed at me. "Of course, you did." Her eyes lock on something lower. "That Omega watch was probably stolen from a victim. If it's real . . ."

"Let me get this straight. Your serial killer radar is going off because I'm wearing a *real* Omega watch? I'm no expert in detection, but I'm pretty sure that's not a reliable method." I reluctantly release her finger, but I hold onto the fact that she never once tried to pull away.

"Money is always a dead giveaway for lady killers."

"I thought we were talking about serial killers."

"Lady-killers. *Serial killers.* Tomato. *Tamahto.*" She nods. "It's all the same thing."

I chuckle. "I'm still curious about money being a giveaway. Care to expound on that train of thought?"

"Money makes people mean."

"Do you know this firsthand or something you've surmised?"

"A little of both. Anyway, what other method would

you suggest I figure out who the bad guys are? I can't ask because what serial killer would ever admit they're a serial killer?" The way she angles her head to the side as if I'm going to give her a meaningful response to this insanity causes me to sweat under the collar. Just a little. *I'd hate to disappoint her.*

"Serial killer conversation aside," I start, holding my hand out. "I forgot to introduce myself. I'm Nick."

She slips her hand against mine, and our fingers wrap around each other. Ah, there's the gorgeous smile from before. "Hi, Nick. I'm Natalie."

Want to continue reading Never Got Over You? Read now in Kindle Unlimited, download from Amazon, or listen to the audio! CLICK HERE

About the Author

Suzie loves a great view of the ocean, spicy margaritas, and spending her free time with her family and sweet dog, Ollie.

New York Times and *USA Today* Bestselling Author, S.L. Scott, writes character driven, heart-racing, and swoony romances that will leave you glued to the page. With stories ranging from witty beach reads to heart wrenching and heart healing, her stories are highly regarded as emotional, relatable, and captivating.

Her books are more than escapes for the voracious readers of today. They are journeys of the heart that always come with a happily ever after reward at the end.

Find her and her bookshop at: www. slscottauthor.com